Inge Diekenga

Between times

Tales, sketches, and poems

Inge Diekenga

Between times
Tales, sketches, and poems

ISBN/EAN: 9783337146689

Printed in Europe, USA, Canada, Australia, Japan

Cover: Foto ©Andreas Hilbeck / pixelio.de

More available books at **www.hansebooks.com**

BETWEEN TIMES;

OR,

TALES, SKETCHES, AND POEMS,

WRITTEN IN THE LEISURE MOMENTS
OF A BUSY LIFE.

BY

I. E. DIEKENGA,

AUTHOR OF "JASPAR GROALES," "THE WORN-OUT SHOE," ETC.

BOSTON:
JAMES H. EARLE, PUBLISHER,
178 WASHINGTON STREET.
1882.

Boston Stereotype Foundry.

No. 4 Pearl Street.

TO

N. H. D.,

AND ALL THE

FOLKS AT HOME,

WHOSE LOVING INTEREST IN THESE PAGES IS SINCERE,

This Book

IS AFFECTIONATELY DEDICATED.

PREFACE.

My publisher asks me whether I want a preface to this book, — a courteous, and doubtless a necessary question, which plunges me into a most uncomfortable state of mental indecision ; the trouble being, not so much whether a preface should be written, as what it should contain.

The book must have a preface, certainly. Who ever heard of a book that pretended to lay any claim whatever to respectability without one ? Like the dome on a public building, it takes up space, and costs a deal of trouble to make it, and is of no particular use after it is made, and is sometimes inclined to be hollow, but then, it is perfectly proper, and — imposing !

However, if it is asked, why was this book written ? I must answer frankly that, as a book, it was not written, but, like Topsy, it " just growed."

Between times, — that is to say, in such spare
moments as an active business life afforded, — it
has been a pleasure and a recreation to turn aside
from the graver duties of the hour in order to re-
cord those thoughts and observations, and to cul-
tivate those lighter fancies, of which some are
gathered here.

As I review them, I can freely claim that the
delineations of character, as here presented, are
not untrue, and that the sentiments recorded are
sincere, and written out of my heart.

To any other quality I lay no claim, except
to such as time and the impartial judgment of
my readers shall discover. If it is anything in
their favor that many of these selections were first
accepted and published by various periodicals, east
and west, let them have the benefit of it. And I
take this opportunity of heartily thanking those
kind-hearted editors who did so much to help and
to encourage me.

The book will appear in the holiday season of
the year. May it add something to the pleasure
and the happiness of that ever fresh and ever
happy time; and that the purifying fascination of
these days, with all their merry cheer, and the

love that they inspire and commemorate, may be
present in the heart and around the hearth of
every one who looks upon these pages, I most earnestly and sincerely pray.

I. E. DIEKENGA.

CONTENTS.

PROSE TALES.

SKETCHES.

THE PRIDE OF GUY ALLEN.

POETICAL SELECTIONS.

CONTENTS.

BETWEEN TIMES.

PROSE SELECTIONS.

I.

BEATRICE CARAMINO.

A STORY OF THE WIND AND THE RAIN.

NASTY, disagreeable, uncomfortable day,
— no doubt about that. Even the old,
gray-headed and weather-beaten janitor
of the Court House, who generally existed in a
chronic state of opposition to every proposition
that was put forth, was obliged to acknowledge the
truth of this assertion, and reluctantly admitted
that it was an unlikely day.

It was the wind that did it. Of course, it is always the wind that does it; provided, naturally,
that it is not caused by the rain, or the hail, or
the snow, or the sun; but, all things being equal,
and none of these exceptional agencies at work, it
is, without doubt, morally certain to be the wind
that does it.

That is, in addition to dust. Oh, certainly in

addition to dust.   For no wind is to be considered
in the slightest degree worthy of a moment's notice,
unless it can make a pepper-box of itself to distrib-
ute an unlimited quantity of dust.   And we are
happy to think, we of the cities of this dear land
of America, that there is such ample provision
within our borders for changing even the slightest
breeze into a most worthy and respectable wind.

It *was* a nasty day.   There! I have said it
twice, but let it stand.   If it relieves my feelings
nobody need object, I hope.   Especially since I
am safe in the house, and do not care *that* for the
wind.   (Be kind enough, my dear reader, to suppose
that I have just snapped my fingers.)   And being
a nasty day through its being a warm day ; and a
disagreeable and uncomfortable day through its
being a windy and a dusty day, it was, altogether
and decidedly, a bad day for business.   Apples,
that is ; and oranges, so to speak ; in connection
with jujube paste.   For when you stand upon the
corner of two streets all day, where the wind has
full power, and the dust comes down in clouds —
when you stand like little Beatrice Caramino, behind a fruit stand on such a day as this, you will
find, too, as she did, that dust is very hard on
oranges, harder still on apples, but perfectly ruinous on jujube paste.

You see, jujube paste melts when it is warm,
and dust clings to it, making it look gray and
dirty, and causing it to taste old and gritty. And
when your stock in trade consists largely of this
luxury, and the insane wind cuts all manner of
capers, and just loads it with dust, why it's simply
ruination ; that's what it is.

Whether the wind did it out of a spirit of mischief, or out of spite, or what not, I do not know ;
not being on intimate speaking terms with the
wind I cannot say ; but that the miserable wind
did sweep around that particular corner, and pay
his earnest attention to Beatrice's stand, is an
abominable fact. Indeed, I might almost think
that he was in love with Beatrice, for she was a
nice little Italian girl, and that he was presenting
her with all this dust in lieu of having anything
better to give her, were it not that I know that she
was too young and that he was too old — the hoary
old monster !

Beatrice tried hard to keep her fruit and candy
clean, but in vain. And at last she stood there,
with two or three tears making their way through
the dust on her little brown cheeks — a perfect
picture of despair. Having no hope left for the
apples and the oranges, and giving the jujube paste
up for lost, little Beatrice raised her eyes and tried

to look through her tears to see how other people were faring. Not very well, I can tell you. For the wind was so strong and the dust was so thick that some people were running sideways, like dogs going to market, while others were holding their hats on with both hands, bumping up against each other and blaming everybody but themselves and the weather for the mishap; and there was one old gentleman who, in crossing the street, was so anxious to avoid an omnibus, looking meanwhile over his shoulder to see whether the horses were almost upon him, that he was running right toward an approaching street-car and seemed to know nothing about it. Little Beatrice's heart throbbed painfully as she saw this. He was such a nice, tall, white-haired old gentleman, just like the picture of one of the saints in the old damp cellar of a home where Beatrice lived, that she could not bear to see him in such danger and not strive to help him. And so, leaving her jujube paste, she ran out into the street regardless of her personal safety, and cried to the old man, —

"Come — come — ze car! you vill be kill! zis way! zis way!"

And the next moment they stood safely upon the sidewalk. And then the car-driver put on the brakes in such a hurry that the people who were standing in the car plunged forward in the most undignified and ridiculous manner; and having done this he glanced around with an air of self-satisfaction as if he thought he had done something quite meritorious for which he expected to be instantly rewarded. The old man shook his head at him and acted as if he was on the point of giving him the benefit of quite a severe lecture, when a great cloud of dust came and completely hid the car from sight. And when the dust was gone the car had rumbled on its way.

Then the old gentleman turned to the little Beatrice. And little Beatrice thought that she had never seen so kind and fatherly a face — not excepting the pictured saint upon the wall of her cellar-home, who seemed to look down upon her at night with compassion for being a little brown orange girl, compelled to sleep on straw and to eat brown bread and old cheese.

"Well, my brave little girl," said the old gentleman, "you have done me a great service — a great service. You have undoubtedly saved me from being seriously injured. Who knows but what you have preserved my life? You are certainly entitled to some compensation."

Little Beatrice moved slowly to her place behind the fruit stand. She appeared to be very much ashamed of herself and seemed not to understand what the old gentleman meant. And if my opinion is asked upon the subject I must heartily confess that I don't believe she did.

"But, first, you must let me thank you," continued the old gentleman, patting her dusty brown cheek ; "you are a brave little girl, and a good little girl, and I thank you very much indeed."

Well, the apples and the oranges could sink in the dust if they felt like it ; and the jujube paste might turn itself into a lump of clammy, gritty mud if it wanted to, and it would not bring a tear to those little downcast eyes. For I do believe if that self-same white-haired saint, looking down pityingly from the damp, low cellar walls, had come down from heaven and blessed her, she could not have felt the least bit happier. At the same time little Beatrice looked very much embarrassed and said nothing. Whereupon the old gentleman hastened to reassure her by saying,—

"Well, I won't say any more about that, and you needn't be afraid of me. What is your name, my child ?"

Little Beatrice wondered, in her simple manner, how it would feel to be really the child of this kind old gentleman. However, she answered, very shyly, it is true, but still audibly,—

" Beatrice Caramino."

" Where do you live, Beatrice?"

" Down zis way," and a little brown finger pointed modestly in the direction of the river.

" A very general direction, little girl, but sufficiently clear for all practical purposes. But, ah! what is this? I am afraid we are both caught, sure enough."

Caught! So they were, without a question. The wind again. Oh, of necessity, the wind again, suddenly introducing, without so much as " if you please " its sworn friend and ally — the rain.

" Heyday!" exclaimed the old gentleman, " this looks bad. What do you do with your fruit, my child, when it rains like this!"

" Take 'em in dair," and the little brown finger again modestly pointed, this time to the large open stairway of the building before which they were standing.

" This will never do," said the old man, " we must find an umbrella somewhere, and then you must have a holiday. Wait a moment. I think I can find an umbrella over there." And then the old gentleman, inclining his head toward the point from which the wind was blowing, held his hat tightly, and hastened across the street toward a bank that stood upon the opposite corner.

Wonderful to little Beatrice Caramino! To think of it! That one who could enter boldly into the dazzling and secluded precincts of the bank — where the gold and the silver were — should have taken notice of the little fruit girl, who looked upon the bank and everything connected with it with the profoundest awe; the grand bank, where the great men of the city came, and where every person who had the golden right of entrance was a king, a prince, or a great noble at the very least.

Poor, common little orange peddler! What a wide gulf between her knowledge and the knowledge of the world! But oh, we people of the world, the wider gulf between our clouded innocence and the pure innocence of Beatrice Caramino!

But here the wind did it again.

I really regret the necessity of referring even for a moment to its outrageous capers, but it did it. And in this way : —

Just as the old gentleman had reached the curbstone of the corner where the bank stood, a great gust of wind brought on an increased torrent of rain. And so fiercely did the wind blow, and so heavily did the rain fall that the driver of a carriage was compelled to turn his horses' heads into a cross street, and drive out of the immediate fury of the storm. In so doing the carriage came quite close beside the old gentleman, who, upon looking up, started and said. "Halloa, Andrax!" and then stood quite still upon the curbstone, regardless of the wind and of the rain.

Really, it does my heart good to know that upon this day anybody had the courage to do anything regardless of the wind and of the rain. Yes, there he stood so transfixed by the sight of some person in the carriage that he took no heed of the storm that was raging in all its fury about him.

Not less surprised was the person by the singular name of Andrax, who was within the carriage; for, lowering the window this person who proved to be a middle-aged gentleman with a very brown but yet a very handsome face, called out excitedly, —

"Montgomery, is it you? Land of the living! do I behold you again?"

"Andrax, I am delighted to see you," said the old gentleman, warmly, and impulsively shaking the hand that was extended to him through the window, "and all the more so because this is a genuine surprise. I supposed that you were enjoying yourself by the Bay of Naples, or quietly resting under the shadow of St. Peter's at Rome. When did you arrive? Where did you come from? Who are you stopping with? How —"

"Beast that I am!" exclaimed the foreigner,

suddenly opening the carriage door in a great hurry, " beast that I am to keep an old man and an old friend out in such a storm. Come in — come in and let me beg a thousand pardons for this rudeness," and without permitting the old gentleman to reply, the foreigner pulled him into the carriage, and almost overwhelmed him with regrets and excuses.

" Ah !" thought little Beatrice, " the good father has forgotten me."

" That will do, that will do," said the old man, carefully shaking the water from his hat, which he held by the brim between his thumbs and forefingers, " it was nothing at all, nothing at all. I'm not made of sugar, nor you of salt ; that has already been tested in Italy, eh, Andrax ?"

" A curse on the brigands ! That very storm has brought me here."

" Indeed."

" Yes, and it comes in this wise. You know when the brigands took us through that awful storm to their hole in the mountains, it was my hope that, please the Lord, I might once more look upon the face of my poor little Lucrece, stolen from me six long years ago. For this reason I kept back my ransom, and staid a prisoner of the abominable robbers. But, two days after you bade me adieu, I heard two of the brigands say that Camillo had

been driven out of the woods by the soldiers, and
had escaped by taking passage on an American
vessel for America, and that to further his plan of
escape in pretending to be a poor peasant, emigra-
ting to the new land to seek his fortune, he had
taken with him a little girl about ten years of age,
whom he compelled by fearful threats to say that
he was indeed a peasant, and that she was his
daughter. From what the scoundrels said I knew
that this little girl was my own lost little child.
Wherefore I paid my ransom, and followed the pretended emigrants. I tracked them from place to
place over the whole United States, and at last
only two days ago I was informed that they were
here — and here I am."

"We will do our best to find them," said the old
man sympathetically placing his hand upon the
other's knee. "You can count upon my assistance
to the fullest extent of my power."

"I do not doubt it at all," said the foreigner,
with tears in his eyes. "It was an offer that might
have been expected from a friend with such a generous heart. But I thank you all the same, Montgomery, as if it had been a complete surprise."

"Dear me," said the old gentleman, suddenly
straightening up and looking anxiously out of the
window. "I must not forget my protege."

" Your protege ? "

"Yes — a little girl over there — a fruit peddler — who has done me a valuable service, and I promised to return to her." And here the old gentleman rapidly narrated the occurrences as they have been previously described.

"An umbrella! Man, what can you do with an umbrella in such a rain as this? She shall go in this carriage."

"I would never think of such a thing," began the old gentleman.

"Beast that I am," said the foreigner impulsively, "I am not yet a snake — I do not sting the hand that befriends me. Who was it saved Count Andrax from drowning when the river was high and the storm swept over Calabria? Alexander Montgomery. And to whom then does Count Andrax owe an everlasting debt of gratitude? To Alexander Montgomery."

"Tut, Tut," said the old man.

"It is so," said Count Andrax, "and I shall not forget it. And so your protege, be she as ugly and as dirty as a cannibal, shall ride in this carriage."

So the good father had not forgotten Beatrice Caramino.

Ah, we of little faith! How apt are we to think, when the storm beats upon us ever so lightly, that the good Father has forgotten us, and like the little peddler, glance ruefully upon our apples and our oranges, and wonder what we live for.

Little Beatrice was surprised to see the carriage stopping before the stairway upon which she had taken refuge. She was more surprised to see the coachman descend and advance toward her, and perfectly amazed to hear him say, " The gentlemen in the carriage want you, sissy. Pack up your traps and come along."

Carefully placing the apples and the oranges in the old basket before her and suffering the coachman to take charge of it she followed him to the carriage where, oh, happiness unspeakable, the good father actually lifted her in and placed her on the seat beside him.

" This is my little protege," said the old man. " Now, Beatrice, we are going to take you home. where do you live?"

Beatrice told him in her pretty broken English, whereupon the coachman received his orders and away they went.

And now, a fig for the wind and the rain. Baffled at last they swept the deserted corner with a moan and a rush as if they regretted having permitted their victim to escape.

If Beatrice had had the courage to look up she would have seen that the strange gentleman opposite her was earnestly and intently regarding her. But the bashful little girl sat there scarcely daring to move, with a vague impression that she must surely be in the company of a saint and a king ; for the fine clothes, the medal on the breast, the queer hat and the stately air of the stranger all tended to produce this exaggerated impression.

When they had passed two or three blocks the stranger spoke, and addressing her in Italian said,—

" What is your name, my dear ? "

" Beatrice Caramino."

" Have you a father and mother ? "

" No mother, sir, but a father."

" Have you always lived here ? "

" No, sir.   We have come from New Orleans."

It was well that Beatrice was a modest little girl, for indeed it cannot be otherwise than true, that if she had dared at that moment to raise her eyes to the dark gentleman's face she would have been startled, not to say frightened by the singular expression that was resting upon it.

" You came," said the gentleman slowly, as if he desired to be sure that he had heard aright — " you came, you say, from New Orleans ? "

" Yes, sir," said Beatrice.

"What is your father's name?"

"Manuel Caramino."

"Has he no other name?"

"No, sir — oh, yes, sir. Aunt Maria calls him sometimes Bernardo —"

"Father of mercies!"

"But he does not like it, sir, for he always scolds her when she says it, and makes her call him Manuel."

Something strange here happened to the foreign gentleman. As soon as little Beatrice had spoken he suddenly and much to her alarm lifted her up from her seat and placed her — little waif of an orange peddler — upon his knee, and even went so far as to press her to his bosom. Then placing her upon the cushion beside him he opened the little window in front and called out to the driver, —

"What makes you drive so slow? Why do you not drive faster?"

"Be careful, Andrax, be careful," said the old gentleman, who had looked upon this scene with silent astonishment; "you may be mistaken, you know."

But the foreign gentleman in the most excitable and unaccountable manner only shook his head and urged his coachman to drive faster. But instead of going faster the carriage stopped, and the foreign gentleman arose and indignantly demanded why they did not drive on.

"Sir," said the man, touching his hat with a coachman's dignity, "this is the place."

"What! this wretched neighborhood? My child, can it be possible that you live here?"

Beatrice said "Yes," and pointed to a house in a row near by — a dirty, tumble-down row in one of the dirtiest neighborhoods of the city.

"Poor child, poor child!" said the foreign gentleman, "that you should live in such a place as this."

Then they went into the house. And here they saw a great many people. And little Beatrice looked around with astonishment, for she had never seen so many people in the house before, even though it was a tenement house in which a great many families lived; and these people seeing her come in broke into certain strange exclamations and expressions of pity.

"It is better for her, he was always cruel," said one.

"She can be no worse off, surely," said another.

"She shall live with me until she finds a place," exclaimed a third, while yet another stroked her hair.

Beatrice wondered what all this meant, especially

since they tried to hold her back and gently kept
her from nearing the dirty steps that led into the
cellar where she lived. Seeing this the old gentleman, Mr. Montgomery, spoke: "What is the
matter, my friends? What has happened?"

Immediately one man whispered to Mr. Montgomery, and another looked at Beatrice and shook
his head, and another pointed at the narrow stairway that was crowded with these poor people.

As soon as Mr. Montgomery heard what the
man whispered, he said to Beatrice: "Wait here a
moment, my child;" and then, followed by Count
Andrax, pushed through the crowd and came into
the damp, unwholesome cellar.

It was well that Beatrice had been left behind,
for there, upon a rude pallet of straw, lay the out-
stretched figure of a man — a great rough man —
whose bushy whiskers, weather-beaten face and
tangled black hair were bathed in blood. There,
beneath the curious gaze of strangers, lay Manuel
Caramino, with his life-blood ebbing fast away. As
the two gentlemen entered, a rosy-faced little man
arose from the floor and shook his head. The
people understood the doctor's action and knew
that there was no hope. A soft murmur went up
the narrow stair, and the people gathered about
the little Beatrice with looks and words of con-

dolence, until they frightened her and she began to cry.

Meanwhile the foreign gentleman had made his way through the throng in the cellar until he stood beside the prostrate man. Instantly his whole being changed. His lips quivered, he grew pale, his eyes looked as if they were touched with fire, his rigid finger pointed at the dying man, and grasping his friend's arm so tightly that it pained him, cried,—

"Merciful Heavens! Montgomery, look! do you not see?"

Mr. Montgomery looked sharply at the upturned face — then started as if he had been stung and said,—

"Is it possible that this is — "

"The brigand — Bernardo Capello! It is — it is. I have found him — God be praised!"

At that moment a woman on her knees, an old shrivelled-faced woman, who had been chafing the dying man's hands, looked up at the excited foreigner who had thus spoken. With a sudden cry she sprang to her feet, and then uttering a strange exclamation in Italian and a piercing scream, she threw up her arms and fainted.

"The brigand's mother," said Count Andrax.

"Then this must be the aunt Maria," said Mr. Montgomery.

At that moment, probably awakened from his death-like stupor by the woman's scream, the brigand opened his eyes, and saw the man whom he had wronged. He knew him and tried to smile, then moved his lips, but his voice was inaudible. Count Andrax knelt beside him and the man looked pleased. Then Count Andrax placed his ear close to the man's mouth and heard the brigand's dying whisper.

"Count Andrax — it is you. I have done you a wrong and I am sorry — but I will restore — I will restore your own — the child — the infant — she is alive — she will come home when the day is closed — she knows not her name — Lucrece — call her Beatrice — Beatrice Caramino — tell her you are her father — take her home — curse me not — for I atone — and Jesus — He is merciful — oh! — the storm breaks — I cannot speak — I cannot see — it is dark — adieu."

And the soul of Bernardo Capello, otherwise known as Manuel Caramino, journeyed outward to the future and the unknown world.

After the solemn pause which generally follows the departure of a human soul, Mr. Montgomery, inquired the cause of the man's death. The rosy-faced little doctor, with a grave look that illy became his cheery features, hastened to reply that Capello

had gone out ; that the wind and the rain had over-
taken him ; whereupon, he had sought refuge in an
old, deserted house close by the river. But a furious
gale suddenly struck the house, which, without a
moment's notice, succumbed before the storm, and
fell upon the man who had sought its shelter.

Having heard the story Count Andrax hastily
placed in the doctor's hand a sufficient sum for the
decent burial of the dead man, and then hastened
out of the dull, close place.   He found little
Beatrice weeping near the door.

"Lucrece — my little Lucrece!" and without
caring who looked on, the noble, stately-looking
gentleman folded the little brown orange peddler to
his breast.

And now the wind may blow and the rain may
fall just where it will.   But we will not fear them
any more.   For they are the Lord's servants and
they do His will.

Not far from the Bay of Naples there is a beautiful place, in the centre of which stands a grand
old mansion, where by the door at eventide there
often sits a noble gentleman, a motherly and stately
lady, and a most handsome, blooming girl. And
at such times one may see that their glances are
directed westward — out over the blue sea, even in

the direction of our own dear land of America. And then the mother will say, —

" Ah, Lucrece, how often we have longed for you while we sat here and wondered whether you were still alive."

" And is it not strange, mother, that we should be so happily reunited after we have been so many miles apart ? "

" It is very singular," Count Andrax will say as he pats his daughter's rosy cheeks — " very singular; as singular as that the wind and the rain should have so much to do with it. In a storm we lose our child ; in a storm we find her again. In a storm my life is saved ; in a storm my daughter saves my benefactor's life. Driven by a storm into a deserted house we fall into the power of a brigand ; driven by a storm into a deserted house, the brigand is struck down. So may we trace God's hand through all our sorrows, and to His name be all the honor and the praise."

And then they raise their voices in delightful harmony and sing one of those sweet Italian hymns of gladness and thanksgiving.

Every year there visits them an old, white-headed man whom the blooming girl calls her " good father ; " and every time the wind blows and the rain falls, this old " good father " persists in running out bare-headed into the storm, for, he says, it reminds him of his little orange peddler. And he never calls her Lucrece, but always Beatrice Caramino. And then they laugh. And they are very happy.

II.

DOPPS.

OPPS was a dog. And where in the world Dopps came from, and what in the world was the reason that Dopps clung to the neighborhood of Barnhill with a stubborn persistency that was truly dogged, and worthy of a better cause, were problems which all the Barnhill population were as unable to solve as the enigma how Dopps possibly got a living now that he had come. For, sad to tell, nobody loved Dopps; and nobody took Dopps in. And when Dopps, in the extremity of his hunger, took courage from necessity, and timidly slunk near the back of a Barnhill house, in the vain hope of picking up a bone, he was promptly attacked by every member of the family; and this attack, being suddenly made and vigorously pressed, generally ended in the hurried

disappearance of poor Dopps, with his tail between
his legs. And thus for a time would Dopps be
ignominiously dismissed from the society of Barnhill. But only for a time. For he always came
back. Indeed, it was one of the most singular
characteristics of this houseless and homeless
wanderer that he always came back. And so
often had he been driven away, and so often had
he returned, that Barnhill had settled down into
an apathetic state of endurance, and Dopps was
permitted to remain to be the constant target
of the sticks and stones with which the gentle
Barnhillers were in the daily habit of saluting
him.

True, Dopps was not a handsome dog. To tell
the truth, the greatest stretch of imagination could
not have endowed poor Dopps with even passable
good looks. And when it is remembered that
Dopps' natural color was a very dirty yellow, rendered still dirtier through long exposure to the
dust and mud of Barnhill, and that each particular
hair seemed to have grown for no other purpose
than to curl in an entirely different manner and
direction from any of the others ; that Dopps's
bushy tail, from dragging in the mud for many
months, was caked and matted ; and that, altogether, Dopps was a most awkward and ungainly

creature, it may be imagined how ugly he was, and how little sympathy and encouragement was bestowed upon him.

Thus Dopps was a most unwelcome guest in Barnhill, and, had he possessed the slightest sensibility to the insults that were heaped upon him, would have left Barnhill long ago. But, strange to say, he adhered faithfully to that inhospitable village, avoiding, as best he might, the missiles that were launched after him by day, and seeking by night, wheresoever he could, the scanty subsistence that supported him.

But darker days were coming for poor Dopps, — days when he was to be not only suspected of being a nuisance, but also of being a criminal. Poor, poor Dopps.

"There it is again," said Squire Hawkins, coming into the house excitedly, and entering the kitchen, where Mother Hawkins was busily at work, " there it is again ; " and without vouchsafing any explanation as to the cause of his excitement, Squire Hawkins gave a tremendous blow to the kitchen table, as a relief to his feelings, and glared savagely at his wife.

" Dear me, father," said that estimable lady, letting the rolling-pin fall into the flour-barrel, "what's the matter ? "

" Matter !" growled Squire Hawkins, giving the
table such a powerful blow that the dishes in the
cupboard jingled. " Matter! 'nough's the matter.
I can stand one, and I can stand two once in a
while, but when it comes to being a regular daily
transaction, two or three at a time, it's more than
I'm going to stand, and I won't stand it either, so
there !" and having indulged in another assault
upon the unoffending table, Squire Hawkins began
to walk hurriedly back and forth, meanwhile rolling
up his sleeves as if preparing to visit summary
punishment upon the guilty parties, whoever they
might be.

" Why, father," said Mrs. Hawkins, " what can
be the matter ? Anything wrong with the pigs ?"

" Pigs !" retorted the squire, in tone and accents
of the deepest scorn. " Pigs ! Can a dog carry
away a whole pig in his mouth — and a live one at
that — besides killing two others, and we not hear
anything of it ? No, they were not pigs. Humph!
Pigs, indeed !"

" Why, father, how quick you are this evening.
Do tell me what is the matter !"

" Well, if you must know," exclaimed the stout
squire, once more giving vent to his feelings by a
terrific blow upon the table, " it's the hens ; that's
what it is."

"The hens!"

"Yes, the hens — the poultry. The bantam rooster is missing, and two of the pullets are dead on the floor of the roost. The dirty, thieving, good-for-nothing sneak of a dog!"

"The little bantam gone! And two of the hens dead! Oh dear, oh dear, oh dear! Who could have been so wicked?" and good Mother Hawkins actually had tears in her eyes, for the poultry were her particular care, and the bantam was her especial pride.

"Who else can it be but that cowardly, mean, filthy, outcast yellow dog, that's been hanging round here now for six months or more? Where's my shot gun? Where's my powder and ball? If I don't see justice done before I'm much older I'll know the reason why," and so saying, Squire Hawkins pounded once more vigorously upon the table and stalked out of the room.

Surely now Dopps' doom might be considered sealed. For Barnhill having been constructed upon that peculiar plan whereby the slightest whisper spoken in its precincts found its way with marvellous rapidity into every house, it was not long before the whole population were aware of the outrageous crime which had been committed. And the horrible suspicion once fastened upon poor

Dopps, a terrible cloud began to gather over his
unconscious head. How fast will a snowball gather
volume as it rolls along! And how quickly does
accusation upon accusation cling to a suspected
character! By nightfall every theft, misdemeanor
or wickedness that had ever been perpetrated in
Barnhill had been laid to the charge of Dopps,
until, in a manner that spoke volumes for the imagination of the Barnhillers it had been sagely decided that Dopps had stolen or slaughtered more
chickens, bitten more children, lamed more cattle,
and killed more sheep than could possibly have
been done by ten other dogs of any age, race,
place, size, disposition or condition. Logically,
then, Dopps was one dog too many in the world.
Clearly, then, Dopps must die.

The manner of his death was not, however, so
easy to determine upon, since from long persecu-
tion Dopps had acquired such a timid and watchful disposition that it was not a matter of ease to
approach him within any reasonable distance whatever. For certain precautionary reasons, among
which may be mentioned a doubt as to the ability
of a Barnhiller to shoot in any given direction
without danger to a trembling and alarmed population, and a consequent disappearance of all the
Barnhillers within shooting range, it was decided

that Dopps should not be shot. Beating, hanging
and trapping were also rejected for equally satis-
factory reasons. Nothing then remained but that
Dopps should be drowned. And it was accordingly decided, after long and earnest deliberation,
'that Dopps should be coaxed to the edge of the
pond by Squire Hawkins' children, a boy of ten
and a girl of eight, and that when Dopps was
secured, a brave party of six Barnhillers headed
by the noble squire should dash to victory or disappointment in the full glory of high-topped boots
and leather gauntlets, and in company with a stone
and string, with which attached to his neck, poor
Dopps should bid farewell to an indignant world
and sink to a watery grave. Tableau !

Poor Dopps ! The first kindness that met him
in his life was intended to lure him to destruction.
Eagerly the Barnhillers watched the lonely dog,
which, uncertain whether to trust the friendly advance of the children, moved very cautiously and
slowly, and seemed ready to fly at the first alarm.

But little by little the distance between them
lessened. Gradually the dog drew nearer until at
last the savory odor of a piece of meat provided by
the children proved too great a temptation for the
poor hungry outcast, and Dopps was caught.

Having thus accomplished his purpose Squire

Hawkins' boy waved his handkerchief as a signal
for the brave Barnhillers to approach. And approach they did with murder in their hearts, triumph in their eyes, and sticks in their hands.

And now, flushed with excitement at their great
success, Mamie Hawkins dances back and forth
while Harry Hawkins holds the dog lest he may
run away. The little girl jumps up and down and
claps her hands and laughs aloud, unmindful of the
fact that she is very, very near the water which at
that point comes up against a high steep bank and
is fully ten feet deep. Well, Dopps has very
nearly swallowed all his meat. Is it the last that
he will ever swallow? The Barnhillers are very
near their victim. The man with the string has
already tied a knot in it and is ready for the exe-
cution. The little boy is looking at the dog unmindful of his sister. She springs up and down;
she leaps back and forth; she skips merrily and
knocks her heels together; her back is to the
water and she is going backward. Are you very
nearly done with eating, Dopps? The squire sees
her danger, shouts and starts to run, and his com-
panions follow closely, but they are still a hundred
yards away from the pond and she but an inch;
she looks up, she smiles, she beckons with her
hand. Another skip, another jump, another step;

her brother looks up at that moment, and in that moment is upon his feet and rushing towards her.

" Look out! look out, Mamie! Come this way! you're going too far! you'll fall! Oh!" And then a scream, a throwing up of two little arms, the one word " Papa!" and little Mamie Hawkins has disappeared from sight beneath the water.

The horrified Barnhillers run with all their might, but will they be in time? And none of them can swim. Dopps has been forgotten.

But Dopps has not forgotten. And the meat is gone. Now then, Dopps! Good Dopps! He springs to his feet, he is at the edge of the pond in a moment, where the boy stands wringing his hands and crying, he looks sharply at the water, sensible! until a little mass of wet brown hair and a frightened face are seen a moment on the surface, then in goes Dopps. Hurrah old Dopps! He nears her, he seizes her, as she arises once more, he turns, and with his precious burden swims safely to the land.

Yes — pat the old dog's back; call him kind names and hug him, and stroke his matted, wet and dirty hair, the old, good-for-nothing, miserable, outcast, brave old Dopps! He has vindicated his character. He has returned good for evil. He has shown that even in such an utterly degraded, despised and hunted creature as an outcast dog there may be something noble.

Well might the brave Barnhillers throw aside their cruel sticks in shame. Well might one of them cast the stone and string into the water without the trifling addition of the dog. And well might they lead Dopps, astonished at this unexpected kindness, back into the village as an honored guest, in no circle more esteemed than in the family of 'Squire Hawkins. And well was it for Dopps also that he was received into the 'squire's family, for during the very first night of his arrival he forever cleared his name and fame of all suspicion by killing a fox who had come for his customary supper to 'Squire Hawkins' hen-house.

In gratitude for his services Mother Hawkins loaded him with kindness, washed him clean, and solemnly bestowed upon him the honorable title, " Hero." And from that time Hero was the playmate and protector of all the children in the village. And if you should happen to meet any of the Barnhill people who were children in those days, they will be very apt to tell you, with tears in their eyes, what grand good times they used to have with jolly old Dopps, the hero of Barnhill.

III.

SIMEON SNUFFLY.

THERE was a little whitewash shop on Bid-
dle Street not many years ago, and not
more than a league away from the church
of St. Lawrence O'Toole, presided over by a gentleman by the name of Snuffly — Simeon Snuffly.
The stock-in-trade of Mr. Snuffly, beyond a dozen
assorted brushes and two or three barrels filled
with lime water, consisted of whitewash and religion. It is true that the supply of the former article
in the shop of Simeon Snuffly was exceedingly lim-
ited, there being at no time enough even for the neces-
sities of the smallest committee of a modern legisla-
tive body. But whatever lack Mr. Snuffly may have
experienced in this department of his trade was am-
ply offset by the superabundant supply of religion
which Mr. Snuffly had on hand on every occasion.

This religion of Mr. Snuffly's being of the
gloomy and oppressive kind, which is prone under
any and every circumstance to look upon the evil
side of human nature, it was a holy nightmare to
all those unfortunate people who had anything to
do with Mr. Snuffly ; and as it was Mr. Snuffly's

business to smear one part of his stock in trade over the blackened walls of human habitations, it followed as a natural consequence that Mr. Snuffly felt it his bounden duty to smear the other part of his stock-in-trade over the darker side of human life. From the continual exercise of his daily occupation, Mr. Snuffly had contracted an habitual gloomy cast of countenance and a way of shuffling along the street that was harrowing to the sensitive nerves of other people, and which bore in its sound a dim suggestion of that coming shuffling when the coil of life should slip from Mr. Snuffly's grasp, and he be seen about his usual haunts no more.

Mr. Snuffly's religion, which was dark upon all points, was especially dark upon the subject of children. What the children had ever done to Mr. Snuffly that he should include even their innocent destinies in the sweep of his religion, no one could tell. But it is true that it was Mr. Snuffly's firm belief that all children who died early were never to enter the heavenly mansions, but were eternally and hopelessly damned, for which article of faith Mr. Snuffly was regarded by the more worldly minds as a monster and ghoul.

Now it happened one evening in September after Mr. Snuffly had had his hands unusually full of business, and had consequently impressed five or six unfortunate individuals with the conviction that they had been entirely overlooked in the scheme of salvation, that there came to Mr. Snuffly's little shop a little fair-haired child. It stood hesitatingly upon the door-step until Mr. Snuffly, at last looking up from stirring his whitewash in a little half-barrel, espied it there.

" Halloa ! " said Mr. Snuffly, surprised into this unusual exclamation by this unusual sight.

" Good evening, Mr. Snuffly," said the child in a sweet, clear voice, so different from what Mr. Snuffly expected to hear, that he neglected to say " come in," and stood staring in astonishment.

" May I come in, Mr. Snuffly ? "

" Oh — ah — yes," stammered Mr. Snuffly. — " You — ah — you — *may* come in ; but hadn't you better go home to your mother ? "

The child came into Mr. Snuffly's narrow little shop, and as it neared him Mr. Snuffly saw that it was very beautiful.

" Mr. Snuffly," said the child, in that singularly sweet, clear voice, " I am the prince of the departed children."

" Dear me ! " said Mr. Snuffly. Mr. Snuffly held all exclamations sinful, and born of the devil, but it was surprised out of him again.

"Yes, I am the prince of the departed children; and they are very sad and cannot rest, and they have come to me and wept and begged me to go back from whence they came and comfort their poor mothers."

"Why don't they go home to their mothers?" growled Mr. Snuffly.

"They are departed children," said the sweet child, smiling, "and they cannot go."

"Dead?" said Mr. Snuffly in a tone of awe.

"Not dead," said the child with a more beautiful smile than any Mr. Snuffly had ever seen, "children do not die, Mr. Snuffly. They have departed from this earth and live forever. And they are happy, ah, so happy, Mr. Snuffly, that if they had the power they never would come back to earth, no, nevermore."

This information came to Mr. Snuffly like a shock, coming as it did to overthrow one of the most cherished articles of his faith.

"But you said they were sad and weeping," said Mr. Snuffly, with a faint hope that he might still rescue his favorite doctrine.

"And so they are, for one reason," said the child, tears starting in its bright clear eyes, "for they hear their mothers' voices sobbing, they see their mothers' tears are falling, and they cannot go to comfort them."

"Why," said Mr. Snuffly, "what ails the mothers?"

"For their mothers' ears have heard a voice," continued the child as if it had not been interrupted, "saying that the children are all dead; that the children whom they loved so fondly, whom they brought into the world with so much pain and sorrow, whom they cherished in their hearts with so much joy and tenderness, have been plucked from their loving arms unmercifully and thrown like vipers into the fire. And they feel that they shall never see their children when they pass into the paradise; and they weep; oh, Mr. Snuffly, they shed such bitter, bitter tears because they do not know that I, the prince of children, am always ready with my multitude of little subjects to bid them welcome when they enter in."

"I am sorry," said Mr. Snuffly, his heart melting in spite of his gloomy nature; "what can I do?"

"Come with me," said the child. It took him by the hand and led him forth, while by some strange impulse which he could not explain he had taken up his bucket and his brush and carried them with him. The child led him through many streets and alleys, until at last they stood before a tall, dark mansion, into which they entered. Here the child took him into an empty room, where the walls were covered with a mass of confused and unintelligible writing.

"The comfort for the mothers lies there," said the child, pointing to the walls. "Take your brush and cover up that writing, which is nothing but the words that you have spoken during all your lifetime. Cover them up, oh, Mr. Snuffly, and the truth will shine forth through all the covering. That truth, when it appears, take to the mothers and tell them I, the prince of children, sent you with it to cheer their drooping hearts and to fill them all with gladness. And as you have bowed their hearts with sorrow to the dust, so lift them up, oh, Mr. Snuffly, into the light of brighter hope and better faith."

And then the child was gone. But urged by a power which he could not resist, Mr. Snuffly applied his brush to the curiously marked walls and worked away with might and main. And, strange to say, as his words recorded there gradually disappeared, other words, not till then visible, appeared upon the clear white surface, gathering as they grew a peculiar light which, shining from them, filled the room with a wonderful and brilliant beauty. And when Mr. Snuffly laid his brush aside astounded at this new·marvel, he saw in burning letters on the wall the glorious truth the child had promised,—

"Suffer little children to come unto me, and forbid them not ; for of such is the kingdom of God."

"It is the Lord's good pleasure," said Mr. Snuffly, as he fell upon his knees.

And then a rattling at the door caused Mr. Snuffly to open his eyes, whereupon he found himself lying upon the floor of his little shop, while a customer stood waiting at the door.

However, Mr. Snuffly indignantly denied the assertion that he had been asleep, and stoutly maintained that he had seen a vision. And to this day he never sees a poor sad mother, who has been deprived of her beloved little one, but what he reverently uncovers his head and brings to her the comforting and holy message from the prince of the departed children. And having found himself wrong upon this particular article of his life-long faith, he has rejected the whole gloomy creed and is a welcome and an honored guest wherever he appears. And from the way in which the children hang about him clinging to his hands and climbing on his knees, it may safely be inferred that the welcome which is some day to greet him from the prince and the departed children will be a very warm one.

"Verily I say unto you, inasmuch as ye have done it unto one of the least of these, my brethren, ye have done it unto me."

IV.

THE OLD CATHEDRAL.

PICTURE I.

CATHEDRAL AND WAREHOUSE.

IF one should chance to wander, in the city of St. Louis, from the river side along that well-known thoroughfare called Walnut Street, one would, in a very short time, approach a weather-stained old church. It is the **Old Cathedral**, whose crumbling front bears this inscription : " *Ma maison sera appelée la maison de prière.*"

They stand there — these words of **God**, imprinted in that ever fluent language — a monument and a reminder of a generation that is past ; when the old French language was the language of the church and home ; when the words engraven on that yellow, weather-beaten stone had the significance to those who read them that the translated words, " My house shall be called the house of prayer," have to us. Time and weather are making inroads on the massive pillars and the solid walls ; and everything about the Old Cathedral bears the marks of age; such age as we can boast of in this Western country — which is still so very young — even to the old-fashioned steeple and the ancient dial; even to the streets around it, which are narrow, lined with dark, mysterious-looking houses, of a long-perished style of architecture — even to Snarlet — even to Snarlet's warehouse.

Hard by the Old Cathedral stands this long, weather-worn, smoke-darkened, dust-bedecked old warehouse. The beams which still support the black and cracking roof have long been hid beneath a covering of dust and cobwebs. Dust and cobwebs also loop in drooping patches on the walls and hang suspended from the aged joice. Dust and cobwebs are festooned about the door, and, when too heavy, break and tumble to the ground, where the years that have gone by have strewn the dust and cobwebs inches deep. Dust and cobwebs cover everything in this old warehouse, not excepting two or three weak bales of hay, that lean against the walls in various attitudes of shrivelled, dry old age. The air is choked and stifled in this building by the dust, which always hovers there as if it were a mist that cannot be dissolved. In short, no discernment can be made of anything in this place except a universal air of dust, and cobwebs, and Snarlet, so to speak.

There is in the commercial world, a dim tradition that this warehouse is a place of business ; faint suggestions being made of feed and storage, upon which profitable combination it is supposed that Mr. Snarlet lives.

Manifestly, though, the dim tradition has but a poor foundation ; since the only objects ever stored in Snarlet's warehouse are the ancient bales of hay that lean against the wall ; and there is never any feed — only — dust and cobwebs.

There is a little office in the front part of the warehouse, separated from it by a rough board partition, from which the paper hangs despondently, and shows the hardened paste in black and ugly scabs. Here in company with a few old books, two or three forlorn-looking chairs, a cracked old desk, a rusty safe and a still rustier stove, Snarlet affects great wisdom and in so doing snaps and growls. In his appearance Snarlet bears a close resemblance to the place, in that he seems to be an animated heap of dust and cobwebs — and old age.

Oh, but Snarlet is a sharp one — and a wise one — is Snarlet. If there is any man who knows precisely what is what and which is which that man (in Snarlet's estimation) is Snarlet. Snarlet, only, knows the secret of success. Why Snarlet in the sanctity of dust and cobwebs, has never turned this secret to account is an unfathomable mystery. Yet that he does know it, must be as clear to every person's mind, thinks Snarlet, as that the sun shines. And that brings us to the thought that the sun shines very brightly on a certain day in June, illumining the darkest corners of the darkest, dirtiest streets, and penetrating — bereft of much of its brightness thereby it is true — but penetrating nevertheless, through the dust and cobwebs into Snarlet's lair.

Snarlet has just received three letters and has opened them and read them — and is, in consequence, in the worst possible humor. For two of these letters were urgent appeals for money due to the writer from Mr. Snarlet — and though the accounts have been long overdue, Mr. Snarlet resents the appeals as personal insults. But the third letter which does more to ruffle Mr. Snarlet's temper than either of the others, is written in a lady's hand, and is marked with spots that look as if moisture had fallen on the paper in drops profusely. In places, where the drops touch the writing, the ink is blurred as if the moisture had mingled with it and caused it to spread.

"Ah," growls Snarlet. "Coming to me after so many years does she think I will forgive her? Fool! Were I a thousand times her father, I would scorn

her. Does she think she can atone for what she
has done by shedding tears upon a piece of paper
and begging me to help her ? Idiot ! She made her
bed and she shall lie in it. I'll have no leaning. I
never lean on any one. She shall not lean on me."

Having thus spoken, Snarlet looks at the letter
and shakes his gray-haired head at it angrily ; then
tears it slowly into bits and throws the fragments
on the floor.

Snarlet's only living near relative is a daughter,
who, contrary to his wishes, married her lover a
dozen years ago and went with him to California.
Snarlet at first had many letters from her, which he
never answered. At last she ceased to write and
Snarlet heard nothing from her for five years. But
to-day a tear-stained letter reached him (now lying
torn and strewn in fragments on the floor) which
read as follows : —

DEAR FATHER: After long waiting, and struggling
against the irresistible impulse as best I may, I can restrain
my hand no longer and am writing to you, to ask you, once
more, and for the last time, perhaps, to take me back to your
heart again. My husband is dead. His means are swallowed
up in worthless companies, and I and my two little ones have
nothing in the world. Out of the depths of my poverty and
distress, and for the sake of my darlings, I plead — I pray
with tears — oh, help me ! You loved your daughter once —
oh, try to love her again. I have taught my children to love
you. They speak of you daily and wonder when they are

going back to 'Grandpa.' But we are so poor – so poor. Oh, father, will you let us starve in a distant land amongst strangers? I am feeble and ill. I may not live long. If I die, who shall take care of them, my lambs? Say you will do it, father; say you will forgive and forget, and all our love and labor shall be yours so long as we live upon the earth. I can write no more. My eyes are full of tears, and I am too weak to sit up long. I can only sign myself,

Your ever loving daughter.

MARTHA.

That is, or rather was, the letter. No more a letter, as it lies in scattered fragments on the dusty floor. In a few days it is trodden out of all possibility of recognition or recovery into the very dust and cobwebs of the place.

PICTURE II.

SNARLET'S SKELETONS.

FIVE years have passed. Not another word has Snarlet heard from his daughter; whether she is dead or living he does not know, and tries to believe that he does not care. But a strange and most uncomfortable feeling has been gaining strength within him for months past. He tries to forget it. He tries to avoid it; it will not be forgotten — it will not be avoided. It makes him angry; and, despite his anger, it increases still. It is a feeling

of utter, hopeless, loneliness. It is a feeling that
reminds him that he is getting older and older, and
that he is alone. It is a terrible feeling that
prompts him to remember how barren all his life
has been, since he drove his daughter from his
door ; how amongst all the millions of his fellow
creatures, the light of love for him shines in the
eyes of not a single one of them. In order to
divert his mind from this gloomy and unwelcome
monitor, Snarlet comes into the light of day
and shows his wrinkled face on 'Change. Now,
Snarlet's eyes are keen in searching for the bad,
and strangely blind in searching for the good. If
you are bold and talk of business, as it is conducted
now, Snarlet sharply picks you up, and demonstrates
the utter hollowness of the commercial world. If
you dare to point to men of standing and acknowledged strength, the shrivelled finger of old " Dust
and Cobwebs " points to men who were once as
strong as they and who have sadly fallen. If there
is any man, however high or low, whose closet
holds a skeleton, old Snarlet brings it out and
gloats upon it — and, when the chance occurs, takes
pleasure in parading it before the public eye.

Still, even in the light of all these facts, it somehow happens that Snarlet's wisdom falls on heed-
less ears, and men labor on, grow rich in friend-

ship, rich in love, rich in material wealth, quite contrary to all his prophecies. And the great commercial world, which Snarlet says is rotten to the core, moves on in its accustomed way and silently ignores the skeletons which Snarlet brings to light, as if, indeed, there were no skeletons, no Snarlets, no dust and cobwebs.

And Snarlet, poorer, drier, dustier, sharper, surlier, and more shrivelled every day, goes surely to his grave.

PICTURE III.

PRAYER AND FLAMES.

ONCE more, recorded by the measurement of time, five years have passed away; swift years, indeed, to those who had no sorrow, slow years, alas! to those who went through trial and distress; but passed, nevertheless, as every year must pass until that last unending year, which will have neither night nor day.

The five years have laid a heavy hand on Snarlet, insomuch that he is bent and spare, and has a very wrinkled face, and is slightly lame and leans upon a stick. Insomuch that walking, which with him is now scarcely more than shuffling, is a burden, and coming to the broad steps of the Old Cathedral he gladly sits down to lean against one of the round stone pillars and rest his weary bones.

It must be a *fête* day, for people are going in and coming out in groups. Seeing them, Snarlet begins to wonder how long it is since he was in a church. He feels unutterably lonely. All his wisdom, all his sharpness, all his independence, all his sordid selfishness, appear like ghosts to his mind and mock him. What have they brought him, these phantoms of his life, to cheer and support him in these his needy days? Nothing, absolutely nothing!

He gets up at last, and in a sudden impulse turns him to the door. The words engraven on that yellow wall, which he has passed unheedingly so often, flash into his mind, "*Ma maison sera appelée la maison de prière.*"

He is not a Frenchman, but he knows their meaning, for a little cheerful son of France years ago, translated them for him, and, though ignored, they have not been forgotten. So he goes in, into the Old Cathedral. In one of its darkest corners he sits down. Its stately ceremonials, its gloomy splendor, its altars, candles, gilt and glitter, and monotonous chant are lost upon him. He only thinks of the graven words above the old church door, "My house shall be called the house of prayer." What shall he pray for, that old man? He clasps his hands over the knob of his stick, and lets his head rest upon them. In all the chain of prayers that binds the earth to heaven, he can remember but one solitary link, it is, "God be merciful to me a sinner!" So changed at heart, so humbled in his pride, so broken in his spirit is old Snarlet that he repeats that prayer; fervently, earnestly, tearfully, full twenty times. Then, without so much as a look at the splendid altar and the flaming candles, he goes out, and shuffles on toward his old, dusty, cob-webbed warehouse.

But here, whatever animation he has lacked, is suddenly supplied by an appalling sight. For a great noise all at once arises; men and boys run like wild; bells begin to ring, and in a moment more the engine dashes by, drawn by four powerful horses, who gallop on like wild, and old Snarlet turning the corner of the street, sees to his dismay, the red flames leaping from the roof of his gloomy warehouse.

Snarlet forgets his age, forgets his weakness, forgets his melancholy, forgets everything, except that in the old cracked desk, locked up in a strong iron box, lies all of his worldly wealth. He has no bank account, for in his universal distrust of man, he would let no one guard his money but himself.

And now! He sees the fire creeping nearer to the corner of the building where the office is. Roused into action by this sight, he hurries forward as well as he can, and before the horror-stricken crowd are aware of his intention, he has reached the door, unlocked it, opened it. Then he enters, and as he does so, a cloud of black smoke comes pouring out. A thrill of horror runs through the crowd! It surges with excitement. They believe that Snarlet has gone in to certain death.

The chief of the fire-department, angry to madness, upbraids his men for letting the old man pass ; commands them to go in and save him, and calls on the police for help. They do try, but are appalled by the darkness of the out-pouring smoke and the lurid light behind it.

"It's no use," says an old veteran of many fires, "he's gone!"

But at this moment another form darts forward. They see him as he springs to the door, and then, like Snarlet, he is lost to sight as he enters.

A deep silence falls upon the human sea, a silence that is more eloquent than words, until, quite beyond all expectation, the young man appears, staggering beneath a burden, (the luckless Snarlet), at sight of whom the strained silence is broken, and such a shouting and noise ensues as is heard

but seldom anywhere. But the box is not in Snarlet's hands. The old man's wealth is lost in fire
and smoke, forever!

PICTURE IV.

THE CHANGE OF LIFE.

An old man, lying on a bed, in a richly furnished
room. A lady sitting by the bedside, watching him. The old man turns and opens his
eyes, and looks around in bewildered astonishment.
The lady takes one of his wrinkled hands in her
own and kisses it fondly. This, more than anything else, surprises the old man, and Snarlet asks
— for it is Snarlet — speaking feebly, —

"Where am I?"

Then the lady turns her face toward his. Snarlet's heart leaps strangely. He stretches forth his
hands. The unutterable loneliness breaks into
sound, in one intense and passionate cry, —

"My daughter!"

"Father, dear father!" cries the lady, and they
are in each other's arms.

When they are composed enough to speak, they
tell each other all. She hears the sad story of his
later years, and of his changed heart, the result of

his decrepit solitude. She tells him all her own story. How, after he had rejected her for the last time, she had struggled through poverty and distress for four long years. How, when it was least expected, she was suddenly put in possession of a valuable mine, once the property of her husband, and considered, until recently, quite worthless. How, being rich and comfortable, her thoughts had turned with kindness to her father. The hope of seeing him once more had drawn her hither. How her own son, going forth to seek him at his place of business, had found him there prone on the floor of his office, in the burning building, and almost suffocated by the smoke. And how, forgetting everything that was past, Snarlet's rejected daughter had taken Snarlet into her house.

"And there you shall remain, dear father, and want for nothing, as long as you may live."

Snarlet begins to beg her pardon, but she will not hear of it; he begins to thank her, and she playfully puts her hand upon his mouth so that he cannot speak.

"You are my father," she says simply; "that is enough."

And so the closing years of his life are bright, and peaceful, and happy. And if you were to meet Snarlet, and would ask him the meaning of his altered countenance, he would take you by the hand and lead you to the Old Cathedral, and, raising his cane, without a single word, point to those sacred words engraven on that yellow crumbling wall, —

" *Ma maison sera appelée la maison de prière.*"

V.

BEN ·SICKLES.

MR. Ben Sickles was a young man of doubtful natural appearances. That is, his features were of that uncertain character which left it a question of some doubt to what particular class of features his belonged. His moustache, though graceful withal, showed a remarkable tendency to turn down at one end while it manifested a similarly strong determination to turn up at the other ; his hair was of that uncertain color which may be auburn, red or brown, or neither ; his eyes were sometimes brown and sometimes blue, or so it seemed, though herein the chronicle may be mistaken ; and his nose, which started out with the good intention of being a Roman, suddenly changed into a Grecian and

ended with the undignified bluntness of an uncom-
promising pug. Yet notwithstanding all this, Mr.
Ben Sickles was a good-looking gentleman and
was "*some*" with the ladies. This was an expression which Mr. Ben Sickles and gentlemen of his
stamp were much in the habit of using, though its
peculiar meaning was only understood by the ini-
tiated. In fact, Mr. Ben Sickles was a young gentleman of acknowledged abilities and made his
dashing impression upon everybody, with the ex-
ception of one solitary person. That one person,
whose obtuseness to the irresistible qualities and
unmistakable merits of Mr. Ben Sickles was a continual subject of remark between Mr. Ben Sickles
and his nearest friends, was "the old man." "The
old man," was the person from whom Mr. Ben
Sickles gracefully earned his livelihood, by being
perched all day on a high stool and manipulating
a black octagon ruler. It must be confessed that
the amount of ink which was displayed upon the
leaves of the books of which Mr. Ben Sickles had
charge was a most extraordinary sight ; inasmuch
as ink-blots and bloated capital letters seemed determined upon a war of rivalry and therefore were
fast filling all the pages, but with poor success for
the bloated capitals who, being weak in the bowels
and empty in the stomach, were fast being out-

numbered by their strong and energetic rivals, the well-fed blots. And upon the appearance of these capitals and blots, the "old man" was wont to hold forth in lengthened discourse upon the duty of clerks in general and Ben Sickles in particular. For this and sundry other reasons, the "old man" was the bane of Mr. Ben Sickles' existence.

Therefore, when the old man put on his coat and hat one fine morning and said, "Ben, I'll be gone till one o'clock, take care of the office," it is not at all surprising that Mr. Ben Sickles spun round and off of his stool with such joyful violence that he lost his balance and plunged head first under the old man's desk. Recovering himself he inserted his hands into his pockets and strode up and down the room with an air of proprietorship which Mr. Ben Sickles never assumed in the presence of the old man, for the obvious reason that the old man would not have allowed it. In the exhilaration of his feelings, Mr. Ben Sickles was guilty of a few extravaganzas which to an audience might have been highly amusing, inasmuch as his proprietary walk gradually merged into a hop-skip-and-jump, and from that into a most undignified and unmistakable double-shuffle ; added to which he performed some of the most astonishing muscular and sleight-of-hand feats such as balancing the office stools on his nose, juggling with inkstands, and throwing knives into an effigy of the "old man" on the wall with a precision only to be acquired by long practice ; and a young lady, who had entered softly unobserved, burst into a scream as Mr. Ben Sickles turned a back somersault and came down within an inch of her nose.

"I — I — beg pardon," stammered Mr. Ben Sickles, " I — I — was not aware of the presence of a lady."

Mr. Ben Sickles could not have looked more confused if the " old man " had caught him in the act.

"I came to inquire," said the young lady, evidently regarding Mr. Sickles with an eye of suspicion, and prudently keeping her hand on the door-knob, " whether Mr. Thompson is in."

Mr. Thompson was the name of the old man.

" The old m— I mean — a— Mr. Thompson is out at present. Will you take a seat Miss — Ma'am that is — I mean — Madam," said Mr. Sickles, still overpowered under the remembrance of his recent athletic performances.

" I don't know," said the young lady hesitatingly. " Will he be in soon ? "

" He won't be in till one o'clock," replied Mr. Sickles, recovering his composure somewhat.

" Oh, dear, and its only twelve now ? But I

might as well wait for him — that is — " (with a roguish twinkle), " if I am not in your way, sir."

" Not at all," said Mr. Sickles blushing like a school-girl, " I don't often keep circus here and it don't last long. Take this seat Miss — I mean Madam. If I knew where he had gone to I'd send for him but I don't know."

" Oh, never mind," said the young lady taking the chair, " I am very much obliged to you."

She was a very beautiful young lady, and Mr. Sickles could not but help wondering what such a pretty lady had to do with an old curmudgeon like the old man.

Mr. Sickles wondering in this manner and with his circus-like recreations thus disturbed went quietly back to his desk and perched himself upon his high stool, from which elevated position he had an unobstructed view of the arena before him where he had displayed such agile tendencies. But the centre of attraction in this arena was the young lady, and Mr. Sickles soon found it almost impossible to keep from looking at her — she was so very pretty. This was rather an embarrassing performance as, nine times out of ten, when Mr. Sickles raised his eyes to look at the young lady, most singularly enough the young lady's eyes were just raised to look at him — and in such cases their

eyes dropped while they mutually colored in confusion. A bright idea struck Mr. Sickles. Mr.
Sickles was a man of bright ideas — though that
wooden-headed and obtuse individual, the old man,
would not acknowledge it and consequently kept
Mr. Sickles' salary down in proportion. Alighting
from his stool Mr. Sickles took the daily paper and
strode to the young lady.

"Here is the paper Miss — Madam, I mean, —
perhaps this may help you to pass the time until
the old — a — Mr. Thompson comes."

"Thank you," said the young lady.

For a little while the paper did its duty and Mr.
Sickles looked at the lady and wondered as he
looked to his heart's content. But at last this ruse
failed and Mr. Sickles and the young lady became
mutually embarrassed again. But what was the
matter with the old man. One o'clock, two o'clock,
three o'clock, and still no sign of him, and the
pretty young lady patiently waiting. At last
Mr. Sickles became tired of sucking the ink from
the end of his ruler and staring the lady out of
countenance, these two arduous labors having
steadily employed his mental and physical faculties
for the last two hours and a half, and sliding from
his stool, the seat of which was brightly polished
from the frequency with which Mr. Sickles slid off

and on, approached and seating himself in the only remaining chair in the office, which was a dilapidated bar-room chair, opened the following remarkable conversation.

" The old — I mean Mr. Thompson seems to be detained."

" Yes, he seems to be," said the young lady in answer to this self-evident fact.

There followed a pause of five minutes during which Mr. Sickles anxiously scanned the opposite side of the street while the young lady narrowly examined the hem of her garment.

" Rather bad weather we're having now," said Mr. Sickles with a frown.

" Rather bad," assented the young lady.

" But then I expect it will clear up soon."

" Oh, yes," said the lady, hopefully.

" It's warmer to-day than it was yesterday."

" Oh, much warmer !" with animation.

" But this cool breeze we're having makes it rather chilly."

" Quite so, indeed ! "

Another pause of five minutes, during which their eyes met, causing great confusion. The subject of the weather being exhausted Mr. Sickles turned his attention to business.

" The weather being such and other circumstances combined have a tendency to make business very dull."

" So I suppose," said the young lady.

That answer sounded suspicious, and Mr. Sickles looked at the young lady sharply. Was she thinking of that back somersault. But no — her face was innocent and Mr. Sickles' suspicions were lulled. From business Mr. Sickles came to politics.

" Besides the election takes up considerable attention. There's Shooks running for mayor against Tubbs. But I think Tubbs stands the best chance. Don't you ? "

" I presume so," said the young lady.

" Presume ! oh, you mustn't presume !" said Mr. Sickles warming with the subject. " You see, there's no use talking, Tubbs has got the best of it every way. He's got more friends than Shooks has and he's got more money than Shooks has. Of course, I don't deny that Shooks is a strong man, for he undoubtedly is. He always was a strong man, and I guess when you get him in his ward meetings amongst his own friends he's the strongest man there. But come to set himself to Tubbs and he's nothing — he's absolutely nowhere. Because, you see, Tubbs is so much stronger and he's got money and knows how to use it. Tubbs stands on his bottom, you know."

"Oh, yes," said the lady catching the last sentence, "except when you turn them over you know."

"Ma'am?" said Mr. Sickles looking puzzled.

"It's much better too to set them on their sides or turn them over on their edges. A washtub soon falls to pieces if you don't."

Mr. Sickles burst into a loud laugh. He couldn't help it. "I was — Ha — Ha — excuse me, Miss, I'm speaking of Tom Tubbs, candidate for mayor Ha — Ha, and you're speaking of a washtub."

The lady looked a little perplexed at first but Mr. Sickles' laugh was catching and she joined in with him. There is no introduction which accomplishes so much as a mutual hearty laugh and so the pretty young lady and Mr. Ben Sickles after their laugh were as unembarrassed as they could be and the conversation, which had lagged and jolted over the rough stones of weather, business and politics, now rolled along pleasantly on the broad, smooth road of good-humor.

But the time flew and still the old man did not come ; and at length the shadows deepened in the office and the sound of the six o'clock bell heralded the time for closing.

"I'm sure I don't know what to do, Mr. Sickles," said the young lady. "It's so late and I'm a stranger to the city — I do wonder where Mr. Thompson is. He was to take me to my aunt's house." "Do you know where your aunt lives?" inquired Mr. Sickles.

"I have her address — 1623 Washington St.; but I'm afraid I cannot find it alone."

"If you will permit me, Miss Rosely, I shall be happy to accompany you and show you the way," said Mr. Sickles, which was proof that the gallantry had not yet been crushed from Mr. Sickles' poetic soul.

"A thousand thanks, Mr. Sickles, I shall be ever so much obliged to you," said Miss Rosely, in such a sweet manner and with such a smile that Mr. Sickles would like to have done nothing for the rest of his natural life but show her the way to her aunt's. It being so late — the porter waiting impatiently for Mr. Sickles to leave the office so that he could lock the doors and go home to his wife and six little ones (by the way, why *will* the poorest people have the largest number of children?) Mr. Sickles locked the safe, gave the inky ruler a parting suck, and in so doing gave his polished stool a parting rub and offering his arm to the pretty lady, left the arena of his athletic triumphs.

That walk was the pleasantest Mr. Sickles had had in a long time, and the more he spoke to the young lady the more he became impressed with her amiableness and beauty. 1623 Washington street was reached all too soon, though the reader may take my word for it that they did not run very fast. And Mr. Sickles had the pleasure of witnessing Miss Rosely fall into the arms of a scraggy, sharp-featured female, whom she called her aunt, and kiss her with a warmth which brought tears to his eyes. Mr. Sickles left, but not before he had received an invitation to call upon her, which he gladly accepted. The next day the " old man " was in a most disagreeable humor, and found more fault with Mr. Sickles during the morning than he had found for the whole week preceding. At last Mr. Sickles in sheer desperation told him about the lady's visit on the previous day. Mr. Thompson's face expressed great astonishment during the recital of this visit and when Mr. Sickles had finished, he ejaculated, " The mischief ! Why I went to the depot to meet her and stayed there until eight o'clock."

A light dawned upon Mr. Sickles.

" Why, she was here and waited until six o'clock for you," he said.

"And where did she go to then ?" asked Mr. Thompson,

" Why, she went to her aunt's on Washington street."

Mr. Thompson groaned.

"Who in the world took her there?"

"Why, I did," said Mr. Sickles.

"I've a mind to knock your head off, for doing it," said the "old man" fiercely and then groaned again.

Mr. Sickles wondered what it all meant, and had an itching desire in the end of his fingers to pick up his much-sucked ruler and give Mr. Thompson a poke with it, for acting so perplexingly foolish.

At last the old man rose to explain.

"The long and short of it, Sickles, is this," said he, "Lily Rosely is my brother's child. She is also the child of the sister of that old vinegar face that she calls aunt, so you see we both have an equal right to her. She's a very lovely girl and we think a great deal of her. But old vinegar face cordially hates me and I sincerely detest her and so we have agreed to disagree and have nothing to do with each other. But now Lily is an orphan and she is to live with one or the other of us, and she's such a good girl that we both want her. That's the reason I haunted the depot all yesterday afternoon, if possible to catch her and keep her out of the clutches of that maiden aunt who never will do her any good, but who will hold on to her like a bull-dog to a cow's tail — excuse the comparison. Now

we are both her guardians, but she is allowed to
choose with whom she may desire to live. What
shall I do?"

"Why don't you write her to come to your
house?" suggested Mr. Sickles.

"Yes, but how am I to get an invitation to her,
and how shall I persuade her to come," and once
more Mr. Thompson groaned.

"I've got an invitation to call on her," hinted
Ben.

"You have!" cried Mr. Thompson, brightening
up — "I'll tell you what I'll do, Ben. If you
succeed in getting her out of the clutches of that
aunt I'll reward you well. I'll give you an interest
in the business — see if I don't."

"I'll try," said Mr. Sickles, feeling as if he'd like
to turn three back somersaults hand running, and
relieve his over-burdened feelings with two or three
Indian war-whoops.

Mr. Sickles soon called upon Lily Rosely and
passed one of the pleasantest evenings of his life,
but felt something like a felon, when he thought of
his secret mission; and every time the old aunt
who was really a kind old lady showed him some
attention it was a pang in his heart. In a few days
Mr. Sickles upon invitation called again and spent
another pleasant evening, and soon thereafter Mr.

Sickles became a regular visitor and called as often
as three times a week. Of course we cannot maintain that Mr. Sickles' zeal for the interests of his
employer impelled him to visit Lily so often. And
if in the interest of this pursuit there was attached
for Mr. Sickles a pleasure which was purely personal,
who shall blame him — and if in the desire to
possess Lily Rosely there entered a third person in
the lists and his name was Sickles, who will be
surprised or say unnatural! or ungrateful! And so
it was. For Mr. Ben Sickles finding Lily more
and more lovable as each day passed by, became
at last fully persuaded that, much as the old aunt
or the "old man" might want Lily, he wanted her
much more than either of them did, and pressed
his suit accordingly.

And what lady could withstand the pleading of
such a gallant as Ben Sickles? Surely Lily could
not. Especially since she had learned to love him
with all her heart — and so when Ben plead with
her, he soon had her in his arms and felt light-
hearted enough to turn twenty-five back somersaults
without pausing for breath.

"Oh, what will aunt and uncle say," said Lily
suddenly, after they had been in elysium twenty-
seven minutes — by the clock.

"Say! What can they say?" said Mr. Sickles.

" Oh I'm so afraid they'll be angry," said Lily.

" Angry ! oh, no. It's the best thing could happen to them. I'll tell you why." And then Mr. Sickles divulged the plot between himself and the " old man."

At first Lily listened with astonishment, but as Ben proceeded her face brightening she threw her arms around his neck and said,—

" Oh dear, I'm so glad it has happened so. Because you see if I stayed here uncle would always be angry and if I stayed with uncle, aunt would be displeased, but when I'm with you (here Lily became a Rose) they will both come to see me and I'll make friends of them yet."

" And if there's anybody can do it, it's you, my dear," said Ben.

Of course the aunt cried a little to think that Lily should leave her so soon, and just when she was beginning to enjoy such pleasant companionship to be left solitary and alone again.

Of course the old man stormed and called Mr. Ben Sickles a traitor and said he didn't deserve his position, etc., but Mr. Sickles easily demonstrated to him that it was the best thing that could be done under the circumstances and the storm soon blew over.

And at last it came about as Lily had said -- the

"old man" (as Ben still persisted in calling him)
and the old aunt frequently met at Lily's house
through her little strategies, and though there was
at first a most dignified demeanor and uncomfortable coldness between them it was soon dispelled
through Lily's gentle words and pleasant smiles and
they became fast friends. And often she has them
both roaring with laughter when she tells about
Mr. Sickles' wonderful gymnastic performances
when she first saw him, and relates the narrow
escape of her nose.

BETWEEN TIMES.

SKETCHES.

SKETCHES.

— —

VI.

UZZLERY.

N the margin of the sea, and between the rapid waters of two rivers, stands a grand and glorious city. And once upon a time, within the boundaries of this great city, far-famed Uzzlery held sway.

What Uzzlery might be was to the common mind of man a strange, unfathomable mystery. Except that Uzzlery was very great; except that Uzzlery was very strong ; except that Uzzlery was very strong ; except that Uzzlery had undisputed power in the city, and infested every nook and corner in it ; and except that Uzzlery was very ugly, and uniformly blighted everything it touched, no other fact was known of Uzzlery, except, indeed, that it was very dark.

Softly at times, and at times noisily, did the billows of the ocean roll before that grand and glorious city ; gracefully the ships of every nation rode at anchor in its harbor ; incessantly the feet of thousands echoed in its broad and spacious streets ; unending was the din of traffic, and the noise of trade, and over and above, and through it all, reigned Uzzlery.

In houses of the rich, where marble meets with marble, and gold is lavishly displayed ; in houses of the poor, decaying like their inmates, and, like them, meagre, dirty, old, and wretched ; in houses of the devil, where temptation led the way to ruin : in houses of the Lord, whose church spires tapered to the sky, in each and all of these lived Uzzlery.

Hundreds for the first time saw the light of day in that great city ; hundreds saw it for the last time, and were mourned, regretted, and forgotten ; and with them, yet not of them ; in their midst, yet neither living with the living nor dying with the dead — was Uzzlery. The government of that great city was in the hands of Uzzlery. The education of the children, good or bad, was its especial care ; the morals of the people, their aims, hopes, and desires, were all controlled by Uzzlery.

Such, in its halcyon days, was Uzzlery.

How it has fallen from its high estate ; how all its power is fading in the city ; how "there are none so poor as to do it reverence ; " listen, ye who would be wise, and learn ; for this is the legend of mysterious Uzzlery.

When Uzzlery was at its strongest and its best, when all the city was within its grasping hand, when all its edicts were a law to men, its chieftain's name was Muzzle.

Great was Muzzle in the city. By what means Muzzle had arisen to this pinnacle, no man knew except the faithful in the bonds of Uzzlery. Yet, that Muzzle adorned his great position well, could never be disputed. Muzzle's office in the city, with the help of Uzzlery, was the important one of supervisor.

In the arduous duties pertaining to this exhaustive office, Muzzle called on Uzzlery to help, him, and forthwith from its deep, dark shadows came assistance in the shape of Nuzzle, Puzzle, Fuzzle, and Guzzle. Great was the city in the care of these five worthies, and very great, indeed, was Uzzlery. It went forth and cast its shadow over all the people. It strode into the schools, and seeing certain school-books which it did not like, took them away, and they were seen no more ; it selected men as candidates for offices, and said to all the city : "These are the men I wish elected ; vote for them." And men, crushed beneath the hands of Muzzle, Puzzle, and their fellows, did as Uzzlery commanded.

Millions upon millions poured into the city coffers, but it was not enough for Uzzlery. For Muzzle and his fellows took the millions that the people paid, and built themselves great mansions on the hills. But while Uzzlery and its disciples were swiftly growing rich, the city was as swiftly growing poor. And there came a time when men became suspicious, and darkly hinted of distrust of Uzzlery.

Then Uzzlery, strong in its own conceit, laughed long and loud. And when the people, growing bold in desperation, came to Muzzle, he blandly smiled, and bowed them to the door ; and when they went to Puzzle, that gentleman confused them with many unintelligent remarks. Nuzzle was silent, and only stared them out of countenance ; while the fiery Fuzzle flew into a rage, and the intoxicated Guzzle only jabbered nonsense.

Then the people, long suffering under oppression, now strong in indignation, rose impulsively, and seized on Muzzle and his friends, and subjected them to trial. And when it was discovered that they had stolen millions from the city treasury, they were condemned and sent to prison.

And so the power of Uzzlery was broken in that grand and glorious city that stands upon the margin of the sea, between the waters of two rapid rivers. And Uzzlery is growing weaker every day; and Uzzlery will fade from human life and human influence long before the people who are now alive shall die. But never, although Time rolls centuries on centuries into its grave, shall it fade from human memory.

For men have found that all the mystery of Uzzlery was only robbery.

VII.

MR. CROOCHER.

RADITIONALLY, Mr. Croocher's office is on Wall street. This tradition, gathering force from the association of a little, dim, back office, with the name of Mr. Croocher inscribed upon the dusty windows, which furthermore bear the gilded legend: "Gold and Stock Broker," is accepted by the noisy tribe that hover near the Gold Board, as an article of faith.

Moreover, it has been currently reported that Mr. Croocher has been seen emerging from this little office at the usual hour, and hurrying on 'Change. Certain gentlemen, however, who have a great desire to converse with Mr. Croocher, and who hover ceaselessly around the little office in the hope that Mr. Croocher may appear, do not hesitate to say that this report is false, and look upon the old traditions with the deepest scorn.

The desire to converse with Mr. Croocher, arising from certain small amounts against that gentleman, is so strong upon the hoverers, that the little dusty office is never free from close inspection, and the gilded letters are the object of profoundest interest. Mr. Croocher does not appear, however, and the gilded letters are fast scaling from the windows, and returning to that vast unknown of dust from which all gilded letters are forever unrecoverable.

Meanwhile, where is Mr. Croocher? and, curiosity thus stimulated, who and what is Mr. Croocher?

As if in answer to these questions, there comes slinking along, upon the opposite side of the street, a gentleman in black. As the gentleman in black comes nearer, it may be observed that he was once a handsome man. Traces of beauty still linger in the fair face, which is, however, scarred and seamed. His beard is soft and silken, but it droops sadly, as if foreseeing some such fate as overtook the gilded letters. The black clothes upon the gentleman, it will be noticed, are fading, and, like himself, display a tendency to droop. As he draws nearer, he casts a nervous glance across the way toward Mr. Croocher's office, and seeing the faithful guard of hoverers on the watch, quickens his lagging footsteps and hurries out of sight. This action, if no other, stamps the gentleman as Mr. Croocher. And so, indeed, it is.

If any one of the hoverers, more intent upon the studying of Mr. Croocher's habits than the presenting of accounts against him, should see him and so follow him, that hoverer would find that Wall street has a ghost, and that that ghost is Mr. Croocher.

For it cannot be that any spirit, good or bad, haunts its former place of earthly happiness or tribulation with more faithfulness than Mr. Croocher. Up and down, up and down, on the pavements of that street of money, does Mr. Croocher wander, with such soft and gliding footsteps that no echo can survive them. Up and down, up and down, with the drooping beard and drooping clothes, the shrinking form is seen to hurry all day long. There seems to be no fire in those drooping eyes ; there seems to be no action in those nerveless hands ; there seems to be no hope in Mr. Croocher's wrinkled face. So Mr. Croocher wanders in his ghost-like manner up and down the

busy streets, hiding in some nook or doorway
when the hoverers draw uncomfortably near. So
the ghost of Wall street wanders up and down,
and finds no place of rest upon the earth.

Once, and only once, a day does Mr. Croocher
arouse himself and become excited. It is when
the Exchange opens. Then the ghost of Wall
street hurries in, and in a few short minutes is
transformed into a raving maniac.

That problematical hoverer, intent upon the
study of the ghost he follows, would be astonished
to behold the drooping figure stand erect and rave
in a most unintelligible manner. He would be
furthermore surprised to see the silent Mr. Croocher's face grow red with passion, as he shouts
hoarsely at the top of his voice, while his hand,
holding certain mysterious papers, shakes violently
in the air. In the event of his allowing his eye to
leave this alarming spectacle for a moment, he
would see that all the room is full of maniacs.
And that, like Mr. Croocher, they are stamping,
dancing, shouting. roaring, tearing, yelling at each
other in an unknown tongue, shaking their clenched
hands in each other's faces, and behaving generally as if they were possessed of devils.

Closely inspected, the studious hoverer would be
amazed to see how all the wild, excited faces had

characteristics similar to Mr. Croocher's. In the flashing, feverish eyes ; in the blue vein, starting into undue prominence ; in the deep care-wrinkles of the face ; in the pallor near the lips ; in the frown upon the brow ; in the startling similarity of the demoniac curse, and still more demoniac laughter, there is a lesson that the hoverer may well take to heart. And when the battle of the stocks is over for another day, and the dreary room, where fortunes are more quickly lost and won than in any gambling den in Europe, is silent and deserted, the hoverer may think sadly of the ghost of Wall street ; and, remembering the similarities he has seen, ponder deeply on that crop of ghosts which shall make of Wall street the dreariest and saddest ghosts' walk in the world.

VIII.

BLINKS.

LINKS — that is, Blinks of New York — is a citizen of the United States.

Such parts of certain papers, tenderly creased in innumerable wrinkles, and carefully covered with dirt and grease, as are still legible, indisputably proclaim this fact. The date upon these papers, which is fast fading from them, or being covered up with dirt, proves that Blinks has been a citizen some dozen years or more.

Blinks, therefore, being a citizen of the United States, boldly asserts the rights of his condition, and upholds his liberty, and, in so doing, gives vent to his opinions.

Were the mind of all mankind the mind of Blinks, or were the mind of Blinks the mind of all mankind, there is no doubt that Blinks' opinions would be taken as foregone conclusions.

The mind of man having, however, a tendency to run in its own channels, regardless of the mind of Blinks, it is quite certain that the great opinions fall upon the ears of the listless hearers, and that Blinks finds fault unheeded. For Blinks, exercising the prerogatives of liberty, frequently finds fault.

Blinks is not prejudiced in this particular, but bestows his criticisms with commendable impartiality. Blinks, therefore, is bitter on the President, and considers him a fool and a knave. Blinks holds that Congress is composed of rascals, and that the government is nothing but a humbug. In all the country Blinks can find no spot of any value, and in all the land no man of any virtue. In the expression of the great opinion, Blinks is known to draw comparisons between the old country and the new, generally unfavorable to the latter. Scenery, houses, lakes, rivers, animals, vegetation, minerals, arts, sciences, mechanism, government, commerce, religion, anything and everything in this sad and ruinous republic, are no more to be compared with similar objects in the old country, than human beings are with angels. Following the course of Mr. Blinks' opinion, the United States is little more than a waste and arid plain, dotted here and there by fast-decaying log-huts, and overrun with criminals and savages.

Nothing is as good as the old country. Do you wish to hear good music ? Take Blinks' advice, and visit the old country. Will you see good acting? You cannot find it here, says Blinks; go across the sea. Would you behold fine architecture? The old world has it, not the new. And so on: Blinks repeats the same advice, the same complaint, from day to day.

Young America sometimes, tired of these complaints, rises suddenly, and requests of Blinks the reason of his remaining in this barren land, and why, the pleasures of existence being so much greater in the old world than in the new, he does not return to it post haste, and grasp the happiness he speaks of.

Following these indignant inquiries, Young America desires to know why Blinks has ever crossed the sea at all, and why he did not stay where milk and honey flowed so freely?

Blinks answers nothing, and is silent for a long time afterwards; but nothing can repress his nature, and he begins again at length to make his criticisms and give his opinions.

Meanwhile Young America, bearing on his coin the golden motto, "In God we trust," goes on in his accustomed way, and, notwithstanding Blinks, is surely growing rich and great.

IX.

OLD FLIPPITY.

LD FLIPPITY is very old. It is my belief that he must have heard the chimes
upon at least some seventy New Year's
eves. The frosts — if frost it may be called that
looks like summer twilight lingering upon a ripened
harvest field — are thick upon his head. The dim-
ness of old age is drawing slowly over his kindly-
beaming eyes, even like a veil, and the old gold-
rimmed spectacles (a present from his wife, now
in her rest, praise God, a score of years,) are fail-
ing in their powers. Therefore Old Flippity,
peering into the growing darkness of his life, leans
forward as he walks, and is becoming bent of form.
and nervous. His cheeks are falling in ; his lips
are growing thin ; the wrinkles in his sallow face
are working deeper, and the clothes which once
were so well filled hang limp and spiritless upon
his aged limbs.

To all appearance, then, Old Flippity is past his
serviceable time, and has no object now to live for,
and may as well grow gloomy and morose, and
bitterly exclaim that all is vanity, and that the

thorns are sharp long after all the roses have
expired.

But, bless your heart, Old Flippity would smile
to hear you say so, and even while smiling would
hasten to explain that you are wrong, quite wrong.
For as to pleasure, why, he has never had more
pleasure than he has now; and as to happiness,
why, he was never happier. Why, do not the children fly to meet him, all along his homeward route?
Do they not hang about him, and push him, until
he is in great danger of falling down upon them?
Why is it they love him so? Old Flippity cannot tell. But that they do love him no one can
doubt who has seen them clap their little hands,
and cry, as they boisterously charge upon him,
"Uncle Philip! Uncle Philip! Here comes Uncle Philip!" Of course, it is true that Uncle
Philip — corrupted by certain young men, whose
most important employment in life is to tell vulgar
stories about young ladies, and smoke cigarettes,
into Old Flippity — generally has his pockets full
of wonderful curiosities, which he is never tired of
showing to the children, and that he is deeply
versed in all the mysteries of "King William was
King James's son," and "London Bridge is falling
down."

Uncle Philip — or Old Flippity, it matters very

little which — earns a scanty living from having charge of two ponderous volumes, which lie upon the furthest corner of a desk in the interior of a dark, long little den on Third street. The dark little den being a bank, Old Flippity's duties extend to the discount and collection department. He is not quick at figures. He is no brilliant arithmetician. He goes slowly up and down one column several times before he dares conclude that the addition is correct; and as to interest, it is the daily nightmare — if such a thing can be — of his life. Still, Old Flippity stays, because his daily bread depends upon it. And the bankers keep him, because he works for very little salary. This reason, in addition to a feeling of gratitude for a service rendered them a dozen years ago, causes the bankers to retain Old Flippity as long as he is able to remain.

The service which Old Flippity rendered may be briefly told. One September evening, Old Flippity, poring late over his books at the bank, with no one near but the janitor, was surprised to hear something fall. Looking hastily up, he was still more surprised to see the janitor lying stunned upon the floor, while two villanous-looking men standing over him were pointing pistols at Old Flippity's head. The sight was such a strange

one, that Old Flippity could only stare in silence.
"Old man," said one of the men, "you've got a
key to that vault. Open it, quick."

Instantly the sense of duty flashed into Old
Flippity's mind. "I will not do it," he said.
With an oath, the leader again commanded him to
do it, adding, "If you don't, we'll blow the top of
your head off."

"I will not do it," once more sturdily answered
Old Flippity.

"Jack," said the man who had before spoken,
"we'll give the old man three minutes. If he
don't open that safe in three minutes, we fire.
Now, old man!"

Old Flippity stood there quietly in the presence
of possible death. The loud ticking of the clock
upon the wall sounded to Old Flippity like the
knocking of the dark angel at his heart. Fifty,
one hundred, one hundred and fifty, — how fast
the seconds flew! One hundred and sixty, seventy,
seventy-five, — the men were taking aim, — eighty!

"Well," said Old Flippity, "hold! Here is the
key," — and he slowly drew it from his pocket, —
"here is the key. Consider what you are doing,
friends. This is a crime and a sin; consider, before it is too late."

"Open the vault!"

" And you will not be turned from your wicked purpose ? "

" Open the vault, I say, or I shoot ! "

" Then there is the key ; and fire, if you will," cried Old Flippity. And suddenly raising his hand, he hurled the vault-key through the plate-glass window into the middle of the street. This action, so unexpected, caused the robbers to look undecidedly at each other. Then their first impulse was to murder the brave old man. But at that moment, two policemen, and a number of citizens who had been attracted by the noise of breaking glass, came running into the bank, and Old Flippity's life was saved. Thus even a weak old man may be good for something. And certainly it does one good to know that in the bent and feeble form of such a person as Old Flippity there hides a faithful servant, and a children's loving friend. And what can we be more ?

X

BONG AND DOGGET.

N one of the dingiest of dingy houses on Commercial Street, where window-glass is a tradition of the past, and only holes and dirty boards are to be seen in places ; where bricks are turning gray with age, excepting where they are streaked with black from the off-pourings of the dirty roof in many a summer's gush of rain and winter's thaw of snow ; where broken keys are hard to turn in rusty locks, and where decaying hinges are fast giving way, there are the store and office of the celebrated firm of Bong and Dogget.

What business it may be by which the firm of Bong and Dogget earn their daily bread, is a conundrum which has not yet been solved. A rash attempt to clear this mystery by a glance at Bong and Dogget's stock-in-trade, would lead to an ignominious failure. For, there being in Bong and Dogget's place only a long and blank perspective of two dirty walls, a dirty ceiling, and a still dirtier floor, upon which there rests nothing but filthy grease-spots and a broken truck, their stock-in-trade is clearly visionary, and not subject to the usual laws of business inventory. From the many grease-spots, on which the dust lies like mould on rotting food, it may be argued that the firm of Bong and Dogget have applied their talents to the profitable trade of pork. A broken egg-box near the door might induce the idea of produce, until a sight of some melancholy grains of corn and wheat before the door, and a straggling heap of hay in the unclean gutter, contain a faint suggestion that grain and feed are the especial care of Bong and Dogget.

What Bong and Dogget may be, therefore, in a business meaning of the term, is a mystery, and will remain a mystery forever.

The firm of Bong and Dogget is composed of Mr. Bong and Mr. Dogget. They have a desk or two in the little office, before whose windows the "Father of Waters" sweeps grandly down upon his never-ceasing journey to the sea. A little matting, very old and very ragged, lies upon the floor; a broken chair or two sprawl recklessly upon it; and a stool — which looks as if it had been in the war, in that two of its legs are swathed and bandaged with hemp twine — holds guard before a broken letter-press. In this luxurious palace, the firm of Bong and Dogget do their mysterious business.

To assist them to master the arduous duties of their daily labor, they have procured the services of Crankie.

Crankie is a round-shouldered, thin-legged gentleman, whose most marked characteristics are a shock of dry and uncombed hair, a bewildered face, as if he had come into the world by mistake, and had never recovered from his surprise, and a pair of restless eyes, that seem always searching for something, which appearance they have probably acquired from the fact that Crankie is always looking for his salary. Crankie is also a mystery, in that no one knows how he spends his time at night, or where he lives. But whatever else is mystery in the firm of Bong and Dogget, there is one circumstance which is always painfully clear to all who have commercial dealings with it. And that circumstance is that Messrs. Bong and Dogget very seldom pay their bills.

Why men, and keen business men, at that, will trust the firm of Bong and Dogget, knowing it, is another of those mysteries by which this firm is surrounded.

Shooks, the collector, has great trouble with the firm of Bong and Dogget. Shooks has an established reputation as being the best collector on the street. But Shooks is forced to acknowledge, sometimes, that the firm of Bong and Dogget are too much for him. The difficulties which Shooks encounters in endeavoring to collect from this remarkable firm are innumerable. When Mr. Shooks enters the office briskly on the first of the month, he is met by the bewildered Crankie with the request to " leave that statement, and I'll check it up. Call in again."

Mr. Shooks, smilingly agreeing with Mr. Crankie, leaves his statement, and calls again next day. Crankie having, in the meantime, invented a pleasant fiction about an unprecedented press of business, which has prevented him from attending to that little matter, entreats Shooks to call again next week. Shooks, in the kindness of his heart, and with a desire to avoid uselessly wearing out his shoes, waits two weeks, and is then referred by the wonderful Crankie to Mr. Bong. It takes two weeks more to catch Mr. Bong in, and Shooks is then referred to Mr. Dogget. Shooks lies in wait three days for Mr, Dogget, and at the end of that time is met by the blunt assertion that Mr. Dogget knows nothing about it, and is again referred to Mr. Bong. Shooks's blood being up, with a determination not to be fooled again, he haunts Commercial Street for weeks, until he sees Messrs. Bong and Dogget and Crankie together in the office, and then charges boldly upon the dingy place, whereupon the inventive genius of Crankie discovers that a bill for one item is missing, and requests Mr. Shooks to bring it down. Shooks brings it down with a vengeance, in that he fetches itemized bills of the whole account. But in the meantime Crankie has vanished, and Messrs. Bong and Dogget profess their inability to pay without the assistance of the cashier.

At last Shooks, grown desperate, brings down three days' rations in a small-sized market-basket, as also a plentiful supply of literature, and announces his determination to remain until the bill is paid. Bong and Dogget hold out two days. At the expiration of that time, they gruffly tell Crankie to make out a check, dated a week ahead, for the amount of the account, less a reclamation for some imaginary damage to the goods, which is so palpable an invention that Crankie blushes, and looks uneasily out at the " Father of Waters."

Shooks is, however, glad to get so much, and hurries from the place, wondering in his heart how in the world such firms as Bong and Dogget can exist.

XI.

BONG AND DOGGET.

II.

IT is now December. Bong and Dogget know this. Indeed, although Bong and Dogget have been known to be singularly unfortunate in the matter of memory, especially in regard to sundry and divers accounts and balances due, which various and numerous tradesmen have against them, they most forcibly and intensely remember that it is December. It is not that the mud lies almost ankle-deep on Commercial Street where Bong and Dogget traditionally do their business, for that is a phenomenon that is at present almost universal in the greatest city of the West It is not that the houses on Commercial Alley — or street, as it is called — are any dirtier, or dingier, or older than in any other season ; for it is not so. They are always dirty, old, and dingy. It is not that the snow is here ; for the snow soon melts, and leaves the city in its one unchangeable and uniform condition — slops. It is not that the frost touches the windows in the office, which has a levee-front, for in the course of business life it

has transpired that such panes of glass as have not
been broken and replaced by paper in the levee-
front have so accumulated dust, and dirt, and
smoke, that it would be hard to tell, even on the
coldest day, whether the frost was on the panes or
not. No, it is none of these that makes Bong and
Dogget remember that it is December. No; the
jog to their memory is something else. It is nothing more nor less than Shooks. Shooks is a collector, and Shooks presses for his money. First,
they bluff him. Shooks will not be bluffed. Bong
and Dogget feel the end has come. All the year
they have been doing business on the money and
accommodation of other people. Where they
made one dollar, they borrowed ten. They were
great on the call-board. Oh, they were wise as
serpents; ay, and with such natures, too. But
their margins go. The luck is against them. Men
mark them, and shake their heads. Men make
remarks to them about accounts long overdue.
Shooks will be put off with fair promises no more.
And the crash comes. And Bong and Dogget
are, in business parlance, "flat upon their backs."
Wherefore Bong and Dogget distinctly remember
that it is December.

XII.

MR. BLUSTER.

R. BLUSTER has condescended to devote his energies to commission. Mr. Bluster's specialty is grain, whereby the grain business has, to Mr. Bluster's mind, received a very valuable acquisition. Following the bent of argument as established in the mind of Mr. Bluster, it is somewhat of a miracle how the grain business could have got along without him. For not only is Mr. Bluster convinced that his own particular business is the largest in his line, that thereby the business of others sinks into insignificance by way of comparison, but it is also clear to this talented gentleman that everybody but himself is doing business in the wrong way, and is positively certain to emerge from that uncomfortably narrow aperture commonly designated as the "small end of the horn."

Mr. Bluster is a gentleman of loud voice, and is an inhabitant of the business world somewhere on the borders of the old Exchange. Mr. Bluster operates in a long, low, narrow, dirty warehouse, having at one end a long, low, narrow, dirty office, whose

windows overlook the river.   Mr. Bluster here
astonishes the commercial world, except such time
as he emerges from retirement and struts on
'Change, or puffs along the narrow causeway of
Commercial Street.

Mr. Bluster's chief characteristic is a peculiarly
audible manner of relating his own adventures and
achievements.   Mr. Bluster is prone to declare,
adding sundry and divers oaths to strengthen this
declaration, that his business is increasing five times
as fast as any other person's business ; that his
profits are enormous ; that he knows whom to credit
and whom to refuse credit, and that, figuratively
speaking, he has a most intimate acquaintance with
the causes which lead to the presence of the milk
in the cocoanut.   When having occasion to refer to
statistics, Mr. Bluster indulges in thousands or
millions.   Mr. Bluster's conversation is of that
peculiar nature that leaves the impression that
what Mr. Bluster does not know is not worth
knowing.

It is a marvel, however, to those who know Mr.
Bluster well, how he can possibly do any business
at all, inasmuch as he was never known to possess
much property, and has comparatively little capital.
But Mr. Bluster sneers and brags and passes on,
and calls men who have been plodding in the

old routine for years, "old fogies." Then Mr.
Bluster, with a high hand, speculates, and boasts
of reaping in his thousands. So the wind-bag
fills.

And then, is it the wind that brings it to them
as it sweeps across the fair broad land in fitful
gusts, playfully uprooting century-old trees, or
gayly carrying roofs of houses miles away? Or can
it be the river that bears an inkling of it as its waters
sluggishly float by the city, eddying around the bows
of steamboats, lazily resting at the wharves and
going on again a little dirtier than they came? Can
it be that the grains of dust bear tidings of it as the
scores of wagon-wheels disturb them in the streets
and highways, or does it come with smoke and
sparks of passing engines that roll across the con-
tinent from one broad ocean to the other?

No! Swifter, surer than all these, it flashes in
an instant over miles on miles of iron wire, and
almost in the same moment it is known in Maine
and California that a panic is upon the people.

There is no time to argue; there is no time to lose.
There is only time to act. And the first act which
stirs the sluggish blood in numerous collectors'
veins is a simultaneous rush to Mr. Bluster's office.

Shooks, the redoubtable collector, is, of course,
the foremost, and demands his money. Mr. Blus-

ter is facetious, and inquires whether he will take it now or wait until he gets it.

Shooks sternly announces his desire, ability and determination to take it now. Mr. Bluster is on the point of retorting sharply when the army of collectors hurries in. They want their money; nothing will satisfy them but money.

Mr. Bluster is at first inclined to swell and become pompously indignant; but Shooks, being equal to the occasion, pricks the bag of wind which is in process of inflation by the pertinent request that Mr. Bluster will either pay up or shut up. After considerable conversation of an exciting nature, Mr. Bluster confesses his inability to do the former, and promptly does the latter.

And it is then discovered that Mr. Bluster has done his business mainly with other people's money. For, not content with such accommodations as the banks have been inclined to give him, Mr. Bluster has purchased largely of various lines of goods for credit, and has disposed of them for cash; and with the money so received has entered into wild and dangerous enterprises. And as Mr. Bluster has systematically avoided the payment of all debts as long as possible, the troop of collectors that now pounce upon him is very large indeed.

The bag of wind has burst at last.

And the Register in Bankruptcy holds inquest on the pitiful remains. Whereupon the verdict is, "Burst through overpressure."

Meanwhile the "old fogies" pursue the even tenor of their way, and leave the dangerous field of bluff and braggadocio to such as Mr. Bluster.

XIII.

THE OLDEST INHABITANT.

HE is an old man, very. You will know him on the instant when you see him on the street. Not that he is so old, or that his locks are touched with silver; not that his eye is getting feeble or that his cheeks are somewhat flabby; not that one hand holds his old oaken cane so firmly, while the other rests beneath his long old vest, or, hanging at his side, swings listlessly and trembles; not these, indeed, for they are nothing but the common marks of age. But you will know him from amongst the hundreds that you pass, by his slow and steady step, as if in man's unending race with Time, he had come out the victor, and had no more need of haste. You will know him when you notice other men, them-

selves quite old, bow to him with profound respect ;
and you will know him surely when you see him
stand before a gray stone house, whose panes of
glass are cracked or broken ; whose door and win-
dow-frames are all awry ; whose walls and roof are
black and ugly, and from between whose stones the
mortar is so swiftly crumbling.

The inhabitant stands before this house — the oldest of its kind, as he, too, is the oldest of his kind
— and mumbles something while he slowly shakes
his head ; what time a tear may be discovered glis-
tening in his eye, and the hand that trembles always trembles just a little more than usual. And
there they stand like two old faithful soldiers of
the past whom General Time has forgotten to dis-
charge.

In its being one of the mementoes of his early
life, of which there are so few existing, the old
man loves the gray old house, for it was young
when he was young, and now that he is old, it, too,
is aging fast.

Yet the old man is quite cheerful in his way, and
if you enter into conversation you will be surprised
to find him smart and interesting in his speech.
He has a mind stored with the reminiscences of
men and things long gone and long ago forgotten.
His memory is a history of your native city that

stretches back for threescore years and ten. And if you touch him lightly and are commonly respectful and attentive, you will have a fund of anecdotes of your father's or grandfather's time that will most pleasantly surprise you.

If you will only walk a little slower, his nervous hand will find your arm, his other hand will rest less heavily upon his trusty cane, the while he leans on you and sauntering thus he will point out at every step some scene of by-gone days.

"You see that house, my son?"

Yes — no — which? That tall, long row or the little dingy house? You are not sure, because he does not point.

"No, no, my son. That large house with the rounded corners."

Oh, yes; why, certainly. You see it. You might have seen it before. You beg his pardon.

Then the oldest inhabitant tells you that there (where there is now naught but banking, draying, commission, noise, confusion and exchange), there once stood a market. A little low, old market, he will tell you, but very good for the times when he was younger; and, warming on his subject, he will tell you with many a quiet chuckle how he and Mary, his dear wife — now long since sleeping in Bellefontaine, God be praised — went marketing when they were married ; how wise Mary was ; how keen he pretended to be ; and how when they got home they found that they had been most vilely swindled in everything that they had bought.

While speaking thus, a hale and hearty man approaches, five and-forty if he is a day, and in proportion stout and full. As he comes nearer, he spies you and accosts your aged friend. His voice is in keeping with his face and figure, for it has a round, full sound.

"Ha, ha! Father So-and-so! Why, I'm right glad to see you. How do you do this morning? But I needn't ask, for I see you're fresh as a lark and bright and merry as a cricket. Ha, ha, ha! That's the word, eh? Bright and merry as a cricket."

The old man chuckles softly.

"Oh, well, my son ; I'm getting old, you know. But, for my years, I flatter myself I *am* quite spry ; and, as you say, bright and merry as a cricket, sir, bright and merry as a cricket."

Evidently the old man likes the cheery phrase.

The stout man laughs with a sort of roar, and passes on, whereupon the old man tells you confidentially how he has often dandled that boy on his knee some twoscore years ago. It makes you feel quite young ; yes, very young, indeed.

"Observe this line of houses, son."

Yes, you observe, and are attentive.

Then he tells you how the fire of '49 swept down this street and consumed the houses by the hundreds, how the river was ablaze with burning steamboats, how the streets were full of crying, rushing, shouting, crazy people, and what a time he had with Mary and the children to escape. If you can spare the time to walk a little toward the west, say the distance of a few short blocks, he will show you houses standing where, when he was your age, son, there was naught but water, swampy land or hilly forest.

So the old man rambles on, and, if you have the time, will talk to you for hours. And you cannot mark a single spot in this great city that has not a hidden story which is recorded in the archives of the old man's memory.

XIV.

THE WRECK.

A Street Picture.

THERE stands a wreck upon the corner of the street. It is a dull, damp, rainy day, but the wreck stands there, unmindful of it. The wreck being, in every sense of the word, a nobody, it is eminently proper that the rain which comes slantingly down from nowhere should fall upon and drench it. Being a cold, damp, uncomfortable rain, with an unaccountable tendency to come from half-a-dozen different directions at the same time, it gives vent to its obstinate humor by slashing unmercifully at the wreck, and runs in rills and rivulets adown his ragged back. It soaks the old, torn hat from which all semblance of respectability has fled full many months ago, and even comes oozing out of the gaping toe-holes, showing conclusively that it has found its way between the tattered garments and the skin, and shows no mercy.

The wreck stands there, however, unshaken by it all, and with its hands in two apertures which may, long years ago, have served for pockets, but which are now nothing but miserable bottomless pits, stands bent and silent, like a dishrag-covered scarecrow, turned to stone. What the wreck is, where it has come from, what its destiny may be, no person stops a moment to inquire.

Suddenly a lattice-door opens in a house behind the wreck, and a flavor of mingled whiskey, lager beer, and sawdust charges upon the wreck, and breathes a little animation into it, insomuch that the wreck rouses from its stony reverie, and, turning faceward to the lattice-door, slowly enters. And soon thereafter a sound of mumbled words and clinking glass comes from behind the lattice-door, mingles for a moment with the sound of splashing rain, and then is heard no more. And when the wreck next comes to view, it is propelled by some invisible force, and flies straightway to the gutter, where it lies in all the wet and slush and flowing filth of Third Street. And now, were any one to ask me, curiously: " Who and what is this wreck ? " I could but answer, mournfully and tenderly, " A wreck ! "

XV

MOTHER BRIGHTFACE.

THAT is not her name. No one has ever asserted that it is her name. It has never yet been proved that she has any hereditary claim to it whatever. The person whose inventive genius first applied it to her is unknown.

Yet here she is, as bright and smiling as the day is long. And here she is — albeit she has never had a child — indisputably our own kind Mother Brightface.

A cheery, bright old lady, hard upon threescore, beneath whose neat old-fashioned cap there can just be seen an edge of smooth gray hair — a gentle, kind old lady, in whose homely face the lines are lines of comfort and benevolence, and in whose eyes the depths of faith and hope and charity are fathomless. A happy, merry, nice old lady, in whose voice there is a sort of music that, once heard, can never be forgotten.

They who know Mother Brightface well will sometimes marvel how her face can always be so smiling; how her voice can always be so cheerful; how, indeed, she can be always Mother Brightface.

For, knowing that the blessing of a child has been denied her, although she has been married forty years, it is almost expected that Mother Brightface should, in growing old, grow gloomy and morose ; but this is a mistake, as Mother Brightface is often heard to say.

Now wherein lies the secret of her happiness?

Ah! my stiff and steady brother, let me tell you what her secret is.

Mother Brightface loves the children.

And in turn the children pour out all the love their little hearts contain for Mother Brightface. She goes and finds them wheresoever they may be. She calls them by their names. She pats their little matted heads and showers kisses on their faces, knowing that with all their grime and dirt they are more pure than many an older child whose face is scrupulously clean. She hunts them up in alleys and in by-ways, and in her human fisheries quite often brings up pearls when she has only sought for shells. She is a party to their budding hopes, she is a comfort to them in their childhood's sorrows ; yes, she is the friend to whom the little children go.

While Deacon Scramm and Parson Poak are busy in theology, kind Mother Brightface gives the milk of human kindness to many a thirsty little one, and in so doing finds her lonely life refreshed and comforted.

Deacon Scramm and Parson Poak are very important personages. It can hardly be conceived how the world can possibly get on without them.

The minor points of their existence are swallowed up in the overpowering fact that they are always at it — really hard at it — and, theologically speaking, resoundingly and poundingly hard at it. The unexplainably long words which compose the vocabulary of these worthy gentlemen are a wonder to the world, and a confusion to the little friends of Mother Brightface. Indeed, so terrible does this bombardment sometimes become that these same little friends of Mother Brightface seem ready to drop from sheer amazement and perplexity.

In the stern conviction that the whole success of Christ's undying gospel rests upon their shoulders, Deacon Scramm and Parson Poak are wont to convict mankind of being worse than fallen angels, and draw a dreary picture of an angry God before the frightened eye of childhood ; and, having created a lively fear, propound certain remedies in polysyllables, in which the most profound research has been unable to discover any meaning.

Then Mother Brightface comes and pats the little heads, and with a few kind words and an inimitable smile, restores the fading hope and happiness again. Then Mother Brightface takes the little children on her knees and tells them stories contrary to the express advice of Deacon Scramm and Parson Poak, who think that stories are devices of the devil.

Then Mother Brightface, kissing the grimy face, and smoothing back the tangled hair, tells them, as only she knows how to tell them, stories having reference to the old-time men of God. And how the little hands do clap when that great hero of the children, David, kills the giant for the thousandth time, and how the little eyes do sparkle when the prophet stands again unharmed amidst the lions, and the three fast friends endure unscathed the terrible ordeal of fire. But oh! it is so sweet to see the little children nestle close to Mother Brightface as she tells them of a little child born in a manger, whom the wise men came to see, and following out this line of history relates once more the gracious story of the Saviour of mankind.

Upon which performance Deacon Scramm and Parson Poak are wont to gaze with ominous frowns and shakings of the head.

But when the little children, clambering upon her knee, clasp their little arms about her neck and whisperingly tell her that they want to be good children, and do, do love dear Jesus truly, kind Mother Brightface has her own reward and silently thanks God.

XVI.

DAVID DAREALL.

AVID DAREALL is a gentleman of robust form and hearty constitution. In the distribution of the gifts of God, the one of health has fallen to David's share, and has made a tall, broad, strapping fellow of him. Thus, physically, David is a giant, and figuratively speaking, may be called a son of Anak.

Being in personal appearance, then, so stout and hearty, David's mental characteristics are in keeping with it, and are also of a robust nature.

David, therefore, repudiates with vigor any puny, sickly feeling to which weaker mortals are addicted ; and stands in his own strength a beacon light to all mankind.

Love, whether it be human or spiritual, is the especial butt of David's jokes ; which, being uttered in a stentorian tone of voice, and being followed by a forcible and resounding guffaw, are characteristic of the man, and cannot help (as David thinks), but damage love severely.

In his attacks upon religion, David Dareall is zealous and untiring — and finds an inexhaustible mine of humor in the relation of anecdotes to the detriment of the adherents to that old-fashioned superstition. Never for a day would David think of allowing himself to be converted; never for a day does David permit himself a moment's serious thought upon the subject — wherefore, never for a day does David fail to heap contumely on the heads of Christians and the Church.

"Look," cries David, with a comprehensive sweep of the arm which includes the whole horizon, "at your ministers. Nothing but a set of leeches, who fasten themselves upon society to pluck an easy living from it. What good do they do? What work do they perform? What equivalent do they give for the money they receive?"

It being mildly suggested that they preach the gospel, visit the sick, assist the fallen, give to the poor, encourage the faint-hearted to renewed and the energetic to increased exertion, and generally bring the thirsty to the river, and the hungry to the tree of life, David Dareall bursts into a hearty laugh, and says, —

"Folly, folly. What dupes you people are! Ministers are fashionable idlers, nothing more, and the sooner you find it out the better."

"And then your churches," continues David Dareall, "look at them. You build them at an enormous cost ; you pack them with fashionable folks ; you extend no invitation to the poor ; you are conceited and stuck-up !"

These allegations being respectfully denied, David Dareall pooh-poohs the denial, and goes on.

"You privilege crime of all descriptions with an insane promise of forgiveness. You quarrel amongst yourselves. No two óf you believe alike. You are as inconsistent as the day is long ; and there are more rogues, thieves, rascals and scamps of all kinds in the Church than out of it."

With which closing accusation David Dareall puts his hands in his pockets, and walks away before the champion. of religion can reply.

The champion of religion looks after David Dareall with a faint, sad smile, as one who would say, " Poor fellow — how mistaken !" and then turning on his heel, goes busily about his work, quietly obedient to the precepts of that idle superstition which has held the world in thrall for eighteen hundred years.

David Dareall, still sneering and still with his hands thrust in his pockets, goes boldly out into the world. In the strength of manhood, David Dareall saunters through the world. But danger comes to David Dareall, and in the strength of manhood. David Dareall struggles with it. But, alas, the

danger is too strong, and, albeit David Dareall
struggles manfully and with all his strength, it
overwhelms him and descends upon him. In that
moment there comes to God a strange wild cry for
help. Hard to be believed, yet harder still to be
forgotten, men hear that strange, wild cry, and
wonder, "Can it be that David Dareall cries to
God? And will God hear?" God hears — and
more than this, God answers. Then the danger
passes, and David Dareall stands erect once more
amongst his fellow-men.

How now about the strength of manhood?

What now about that idle superstition?

Not answering these questions, David Dareall, in
the pride of health, walks on once more. In the
pride of health he wanders through the slums and
alleys of the city, where disease takes hardy root
and desperately holds fast ; where air is but another
name for poison, and where the black cart from the
potter's field has far too much to do. David Dareall wanders here, and in the pride of health inveighs
against religion, charging it with all the wretched-
ness and want, poverty, disease and crime, that have
their woful and unhealthy growth in this sad place
— saying that if the Christian people would attend
to these waste places, and not spend their time in
singing psalms and useless works like that, it would
be better for the world.

David Dareall saunters once too often in this place. The evening star beholds him well and strong and in the pride of health. The morning star beholds him lying on his bed, fever burning in his cheeks and flaming in his eye, and when the evening star again beholds him he is very low. Lower still as night succeeds to day — lower, lower still as day succeeds to night; and soon a thin, attenuated form lies on the bed — nigh, very nigh, to death.

What wavers feebly in the sick man's room, and ascends unto the Father's throne? What! has the fever touched his brain, that David Dareall prays to God for health? And will God answer a crazy prayer at the eleventh hour?

God answers surely. And the morning and the evening stars behold the sick man slowly getting strong again, and singing praise, and sometimes falling on his knees and giving thanks.

How now about the pride of health?

What now about that idle superstition?

David Dareall answers nothing to these questions. But he is heard to murmur fervently and frequently, " How weak — even in the strength of manhood and the pride of health — how very weak I am."

And at the champion of religion David Dareall sneers no more.

XVII

SISTER JANE.

EW roses gather in the path of sister Jane. And when, from time to time, she stoops to touch the few that bloom around her, it happens that the thorns are very sharp beneath their pretty leaves, or, lacking thorns, they wither with a touch, and die.

Clouds very often hide the sun from sister Jane; or, having shed their rain upon the earth, mist rises from the waters, and she cannot see. Such happiness as she has known is of the very dim and distant past, and has been in other minds long, long ago forgotten. But to their memories sister Jane clings fondly. For these memories are to her like flowers pressed between the · leaves of books, which, albeit they are faded, perfumeless, and dead, are cherished tenderly, in honor of the vanished faces that will return upon the earth no more, no more.

And yet the search to find a line of sorrow or a trace of care on sister Jane's smooth brow must needs be very deep, aye, very deep and keen, to be successful ; and hope to find a look of trouble in the soft, blue eyes, or in the quiet, gentle face, would meet with disappointment. For there is that within her, mysterious and unexplainable as it may be, which sheds an air of calm contentment all around. And in her trustful eyes there is a light that none can see, and, having seen, forget.

It is the light of Faith.

Of all her dear ones, sister Jane has none about her now — not one. Some sleep peacefully in the quiet city of the dead, where the perfume of sweet flowers under weeping willows gives proof of sister Jane's kind care. Some rest beneath the moaning waters of the sea. Some are covered by the desert's burning sand. And some — God only knows — for to the world and sister Jane they have been lost forever.

Then why is sister Jane so calm and so contented? And how is it the light of faith shines in her eye so brightly? Come, follow me into a room, not finely furnished, yet, notwithstanding, neat and clean. Draw nearer, softly, to the woman reading at the table. Glance carefully over the bending form, and look at the words upon which the trustful eyes are fixed, and read, as they are reading, —

"Come unto me, all ye that labor and are heavy laden, and I will give you rest. Take my yoke upon you and learn of me; for I am meek and lowly in heart; and ye shall find rest to your souls. For my yoke is easy and my burden is light."

Then watch the woman slowly fall upon her knees and gratefully accept the gracious invitation. Hear the soft prayer for help and guidance; see how there is a beauty in the silent quiet face, and behold how very, very bright the light of faith shines in the trustful eyes.

Then follow warily, as rising from her knees she leaves the room, and goes where many a tender lady would not dare to go. See how she finds the bedside of the poor, and lifts up the desponding sick into the strength of brighter hopes — how she makes her way amongst the stricken and the fallen who, finding sympathy in her kind earnestness, come out from brooding over sorrow, even through the strength of that sweet quiet face, and that undying light of faith. See her as she wanders through the very scum and offal of mankind, and behold her as she brings forth all the best of human feelings where common charity could only find the worst, and then observe her as the children cling about her, and will not let her go — and you will know why sister Jane is so contented and so happy. But more than this the mystery will be made clear, by hearing sister Jane, as kneeling by the bedside when the day is over, she thanks God for all His many mercies, and murmurs softly: "One day nearer! Oh, I thank Thee, Heavenly Father, that the days are growing less and less that keep me from Thee, that keep me from my loved ones ; that surely, surely, I am nearing heaven. Oh, Father — dear, kind Father — make me strong to bear the joy of meeting Thee, give me strength that I may see the glory of my Saviour, and not die ; and, oh, up-hold me, that I faint not when I clasp my loved ones in my arms once more. For I praise Thy holy name, my Father ; my heart is bound to Thee." And just before the lamp-light is extinguished, a wavering, trembling, yet withal a pleasant voice may be heard singing, —

" One sweetly solemn thought comes to me o'er and o'er.
I'm nearer my home to-day than ever I've been before ;
I'm nearer my home, nearer my home, nearer my home
   to-day.
Yes, nearer my home in heaven to-day than ever I've
   been before."

XVIII

LITTLE TODDLER.

ITTLE TODDLER is a gentleman in petticoats.

They who are supposed to know these secret matters aver that age is creeping fast on Little Toddler, and that if he keeps on so bravely he will soon discard the youthful petticoats and don the manly pants ; and there are even rumors of a plot between that angel of mysterious things, namely : Little Toddler's mamma and the genius of the shears, viz : Miss Snipps, the dressmaker, to the effect that the forthcoming pants shall be of rich dark blue, and that the buttons shall be of the brightest brass the market can afford. Moreover it is certain, documentary proof being compressed between the pages of the family Bible, that Little Toddler is just a month and two days more than three years old.

It is then not strange that, in the dignity of his advancing years, Little Toddler should be rather enterprising in his disposition, and of an inquiring mind, and that in the pursuit of his investigations, instituted through these traits of character, he should frequently press forward into danger.

Not only does Little Toddler press forward into danger, but he is often found to plunge into it in the most abrupt and unexpected manner. And, in so doing, he brings trepidation and alarm amongst the angels.

These angels, hovering about the path of Little Toddler, faithfully protect him in his daily life. Indeed, if it were not for these angels, Little Toddler might himself have been a little angel long ago.

First and foremost of these angels, ranking number one, stands Little Toddler's mamma.

Surely in the list of Heaven's angels there are none more sweet or true. Surely this dear angel is a godsend in the life of Little Toddler. Surely, surely, there is beauty everywhere when she is near. What angel is so vigilant in watching Little Toddler, lest in venturing too near that dangerous precipice, the staircase, he tumble down the steps? Who rescues him from drowning in a tub, and catches him in time as he is rashly plunging through the window? Who hides the concentrated lye lest Little Toddler find it, and saves him from his enemy, the cat? And in whose arms, so dear and soft, is there such perfect rest? Who calls him " mamma's little pet," and smothers him with kisses ; and who sings to him that potent lullaby, " Rock-a-by, baby, in the tree-top," until Little Toddler gets quite drowsy, and, at peace with all the world, falls dreamily asleep? Ah, darling angel! sweet, dear mamma! God ordains that when the other angels have been all forgotten, this dear one shall yet be bright in Little Toddler's memory.

And then there is the angel papa. A great tall, sturdy angel, who thinks a deal of Little Toddler, and rides 'him on his knee — who calls him "little man," and laughs aloud when Little Toddler tries to speak. An angel with a covering of hair upon his face which sticks and tickles Little Toddler when the angel tries to kiss him. An angel with a mystery, in that he goes each morning out into that vague and boundless world beyond the garden gate, which Little Toddler has an intense desire to explore. Yet a grand, good angel, in that he reappears at evening with a mine of treasures, consisting of sweetmeats, dogs, cats, mimic soldiers, jumping-jacks, Chinese puzzles, and the like, in his unfathomable pocket.

Then there is angel brother John, who holds Little Toddler on old Rover's back, and rides him up and down the yard. And angel Margaret, the housemaid, who plays with Little Toddler while she makes the beds. And angel Bridget in the kitchen, who is on especial duty to prevent the red-hot stove from scorching him, and many other angels, all of whom have watch and ward o'er Little Toddler.

And so it is that Little Toddler, although venturesome and bold, is guarded and protected, and has so far escaped the dangers which have threatened him.

Whether there is ever any speculation in the mind of Little Toddler as to how the angels who protect him are themselves protected, cannot at present be determined, as Little Toddler has not yet learnt his mother tongue. Yet, he is very wise and learning fast, and we shall know quite soon what Little Toddler thinks about it.

Pending which it may be well to ask ourselves this question : Are there any angels guarding us as there are angels guarding Little Toddler? Are the dangers that so often threaten us made powerless by unseen power greater than our own?

It must be so. For we are naught but grown-up Little Toddlers, after all — blindly rushing into danger that we cannot see — craving for the things that cannot help but do us harm, and daily being rescued by the unseen angels. Therefore let us have, like Little Toddler, an unfaltering faith in our good Father in the unseen world beyond our narrow little sphere. And may He find us, Little Toddlers, glad and ready to receive Him when He comes.

BETWEEN TIMES.

THE PRIDE OF GUY ALLEN.

THE PRIDE OF GUY ALLEN.

THE VILLAGE.

MONG the villages which share
New England's ever watchful care, —
Where taste and pardonable pride
Her cottages have beautified,
In clusters fair, adorning still
The level land, or vale or hill;
Where the home-love, which freely all
Surrenders at its country's call,
Here in its beauty is displayed
In gardens trim and walks well laid,
In orchards full and roadways wide,
And happy homes on every side;
While, set against the deep blue sky,
The slender church-spire greets the eye, —
None could more fair or pleasant be
Than one which looked upon the sea.

Oft when the night had gathered dark
About their tempest-driven bark,
Imperilled mariners had seen,
With joy, the village lights serene,
And, guided by these beacons pure,
In peaceful haven rode secure.
The traveller, too, whose spirit yearned,
As from his wanderings he returned,
Rejoiced those well-known sounds to near,
Which he had often longed to hear,
As, pressing hard his tired feet,
He sped his early friends to meet,
Sure, though the world remembered not,
That here he had not been forgot.
Here rose the sound of church-bells clear,
By distance mellowed to the ear,
Sweet-toned and dying soft away,
Far landward — farther o'er the bay ;
Here rose the smith's melodious song,
The farm-boy's echo — full and long,
The country wagon's creaking noise,
The shouts of village girls and boys,
The cattle lowing from the pool,
The drowsy murmur of the school ; —
All, as the wanderer nearer drew,
A conscious spell around him threw ;

Or, when the Sabbath brought its peace,
And caused the sounds of toil to cease —
When the low chant or sacred psalm
Broke the sweet Sabbath's holy calm ;
And once again, with earnest face,
The pastor preached the word of grace ;
How happy he, who from the scene,
By sea and land had parted been,
Once more the modest church to view,
The square, high-backed, old-fashioned pew
To see, albeit older grown,
Some of the faces he had known,
And, grateful for the dangers past,
Thank God that he was home at last.

THE HOMESTEAD.

SOME stranger, whose observant eye
Each noted landmark sought to spy,
Might in this peaceful village find
Much to enrich his curious mind ;
But most of all his glance would stray
Where, back from the accustomed way,
Midst humbler cottages of wood,
A more pretentious mansion stood.
'Twas built of stone of wide-spread fame,

Bore on the door its owner's name ;
Bright windows, many-paned and wide,
Let in the light on every side ;
Square walls, all covered o'er with vine,
Broad porches, decked with roses fine,
A green lane, through a stately grove
Of elm trees, interlaced above ;
To right and left, fair beds of flowers ;
In sheltered places, rustic bowers,
And a wide lawn, whose velvet green
Might rouse the envy of a queen.
All these, with fields of waving grain,
That filled the wide and fruitful plain,
Combined, in beauties rich and rare,
To make a homestead passing fair.
Here lived Guy Allen ; well could he
The village Crœsus claim to be.

GUY ALLEN.

GUY ALLEN was proud, for he could trace
Through centuries his ancestral race :
On vast estate and castle stone,
The light of generations shone ;
And though to these, or titled name,
New England born, he ne'er laid claim,

He felt that through his pulses flowed
The crimson tide of noble blood.
This gave his brow its haughty curve ;
This tinged his mien with cold reserve ;
Gave to his feet their haughty tread,
Its stately bearing to his head ;
And though he would have scorned to own
Allegiance to an earthly throne,
And though, were danger to assail
His native land, he would not fail
To faithfully defend its laws,
Or shed his blood in freedom's cause,
Guy Allen could not quite forget
His family name and coronet.
Of many sons he had been one,
But, as the years their course had run,
The brothers whom he dearly loved,
By death, all certain, were removed :
In slow consumption's sure decay
His wife had early passed away ;
And now, an only daughter dear
Remained his growing age to cheer.

MAY ALLEN.

May Allen was fair as fair could be,
The pride of village maids was she,
Beauty, and youth, and health, gave grace
To every feature of her face.
With just enough of native pride
To mark the sterner parent's side —
While even this would melt before
The touching stories of the poor —
Her gentler nature still was shown
In modest mien and gentle tone:
And if at times her youth found vent
In pure and harmless merriment,
The while her happy speech was full
Of humor irrepressible,
She guarded well her flashing wit
Lest it some tender heart might hit,
Which, sorely grieved, might from her turn
And with resentment hotly burn;
With glances bright, and sunny smiles
She spoke, while these unconscious wiles
Into her fast increasing train
Drew many a love-lorn village swain.

Guy Allen loved his daughter well,
More than that stern man chose to tell.

He heard with fond paternal pride
Her praises echoed far and wide,
And though his love was not displayed .
By any outward sign he made,
His feeling grew the more intense
Because devoid of warm pretence.
Yet the great love that held her dear
Was not without its constant fear :
For, as he marked her growing charms, ·
Ofttimes distrust and vague alarms
His mind disturbed, and sent a dart
Of apprehension to his heart,
Lest, tempted by her gentle worth,
Some daring lad of humble birth,
Whose only fortune at command
Was in his brain and in his hand,
With thoughtless and audacious fire
Might to her heart and hand aspire.
Wherefore Guy Allen was imbued
At times with deep solicitude,
And watched with keen suspicious eye
Each visitor who ventured nigh.
For he was proud — and he had said :
" If e'er my daughter dares to wed
With one beneath her station born
She shall be heiress of my scorn :

Henceforth and ever unto me
An utter stranger she shall be ;
I will not know her though she pleads
For pardon on her bended knees ;
Nor shall she pass my threshold o'er
Although in rags she seeks my door."
And thus to her : " Remember, girl,
You are descended from an earl ;
The names of our illustrious line
Undimmed through generations shine.
Do not forget your birth and place,
You are the last of all your race,
And when you wed, as wed you will,
Your father's counsel follow still."

Then clinging to her father's side
May Allen laughingly replied :
" But, father dear, where shall I find
A lover worthy to your mind ?
For where is he who dares to boast,
In all New England's dented coast,
A title, or demand the rights
That Europe gives to lords and knights ?
'Twere but a foolish thought to aim
In this free land at pride of name."

Then on his daughter looking down,
With half a smile, and half a frown,

Guy Allen said : " The land is free,
And knows no pomp of heraldry
(And I am glad, for courts and kings
Are oftentimes but hollow things) ;
But I will have no village boor
Or penniless lad your love allure —
Nor would I have you sell your love ;
Choose wisely — all your feelings prove —
Turn from the man who does not clasp
Your very soul within his grasp —
But one of low degree in vain
May hope my favor to obtain ;
And if against my will you wed
My love to hate shall turn instead,
And from that day of fell disgrace
You ne'er shall see your father's face."

But who can say when love begins,
When first the inner soul it wins,
What mortal check its fond desire,
Or quench at will its holy fire ?
And who can mark the fateful hour
When first it slowly gathers power ?
Not the quick passion which upstarts
A feverish flame in fickle hearts,
But the strong fire, long burning low
Until, above its hot red glow,

Subduing all, it bursts at length
From heart to heart with heavenly strength,
And, heeding naught that stands before,
Burns stronger, brighter, evermore;
Until, for them to whom 'tis given,
It gilds the very gates of heaven.
Full many an unseen subtle thread
Of circumstance has slowly led
The heart blindfolded to its mate,
Predestined by unerring fate.
For love its course will still pursue
Despite what mortal power may do,
And in its golden fetters bind
Hearts which for union were designed.

RICHARD LEIGH.

Now in the village there was one
Who had his life-work just begun; .
A youth he was of comely face,
Of supple limb and manly grace,
And for his sterling parts held dear
Throughout the country, far and near:
But he was poor and could not claim
Kinship to noble lord or dame;

He lacked the wealth which might disguise
The lack of " blood " in Allen's eyes.
Wherefore Guy Allen would not bend
To greet him by the name of friend,
And scarcely deigned to show that he
Knew the young doctor, Richard Leigh ;
Who, from all envious thoughts exempt,
Unmoved by Allen's cold contempt,
Labored in his appointed way
In faithful toil from day to day.

THE RESCUE.

BUT chance will oft at length decide
In spite of human will and pride.
And shall we call it simply chance ?
May it not well be Providence
Which from the tangled thread of life,
With knots and imperfections rife,
Draws forth the perfect strands, to be
Woven in beauteous harmony ?
And so, upon a wintry day,
While trudging o'er the snow-decked way,
Richard suddenly heard a shout,
And, turning instantly about,

Beheld a frightened, frantic steed
Dashing along with headlong speed,
Furious before the frail, light sleigh
In which, alone, sat gentle May,
Holding the reins with fingers numb,
In speechless terror pale and dumb.
But little time was there to think,
For they were close upon the brink
Of a rude chasm, deep and wide,
From which — abruptly turned aside —
The road a new direction took,
Following, with many a curve and crook,
The precipice for half a mile,
Where danger threatened all the while.
Were the mad steed with his light load
To dash into this dangerous road
The dullest mind could well foresee
How sad the awful end might be ;
For swerving from that winding path
Meant sure and instantaneous death.

He saw the danger where he stood ;
It shocked his heart and chilled his blood.
One moment in suspense supreme
He waited — then as from a dream
Of horrid import just awaked,
He forward sprang with limbs that quaked

But firm of will and clear of eye,
And with a sharp, commanding cry,
Caught with one hand the horse's mane,
And with the other grasped the rein,
And thus, in almost fatal wise,
Was dragged before May Allen's eyes.
But the mad steed this added strain
Not many moments could maintain,
And soon he faltered in his race,
Slackened his fierce, impetuous pace,
Until, subdued by voice and strength,
Trembling and spent, he stopped at length.

A sturdy farmer and his son,
Who witnessed how the deed was done,
Hastened their kindly aid to lend
To him who oft had been their friend ;
And when they quickly reached her side
Who thus had ta'en this fearful ride,
They saw a pale, unconscious face
Whereon great fear had left its trace.
While still the slender hands tight clasped
The reins, with all their might held fast.

THE REWARD.

With gentle haste and tender care,
Wrapped in warm furs, they carried her
Back to her father's home, where soon
She wakened from her deathlike swoon.
Then to depart was Richard fain,
But May compelled him to remain,
While her great gratitude found vent
In tears and glances eloquent.
And when to Allen it was told,
With strange emotions manifold
He thanked the youth who thus could brave
Danger and death a life to save.
And though the old, inherent pride
Was far from being satisfied,
Still one who had so well preserved
His daughter's life in truth deserved
Some recognition more than he
Had yet vouchsafed to Richard Leigh.
For, though proud-hearted, he was just;
And, breaking through the haughty crust
Of self-reserve and cold command,
He grasped the young physician's hand,

And thanked him — urged him to remain —
And begged him oft to come again,
And pledged himself in every way
His debt of service to repay.

LOVE'S BEGINNING.

THEN Richard went away well pleased,
With a light step and a heart eased
Of a great burden which had pressed
Like a huge stone upon his breast.
For he had worshipped from afar
With secret love the village star;
A love deep hid within his heart
While they by pride were kept apart.
Sweet were his dreams that winter night,
And beautiful the hope whose light,
Erstwhile but dimly shining, now
Set its bright seal upon his brow;
While from that day, with joy renewed,
He labored on in happier mood,
And oft turned, when his tasks were o'er.
His willing feet towards Allen's door,
Where, of all hearts, at least beat one
With his in gentle unison.

For men will seek and men will find
The tender love of womankind,
Which still o'er all the world holds sway
In the same dear resistless way,
Which has controlled, since earth began,
The hopes and destinies of man.

Guy Allen was not quite content.
He felt that some impediment
Should in the young man's path be thrown.
But recognition had been shown
To him in public word and act,
And 'twere unmanly to retract
His favor for the slender cause,
Which bare suspicion dimly draws.
But, when alone with May, his fear
Broke forth in caution sharp and clear.
Little indeed Guy Allen knew
When first that fluttering feeling grew
Which soon, transcending every thought,
Its power in May's sweet spirit wrought.
And when, at last, before his eyes,
His fears he came to realize,
He felt, with blind and bitter pain,
That all his caution had been vain.

ALLEN'S ANGER.

BUT now at length the time had come
When the desire, which had been dumb
So long, could not itself contain,
Nor longer voiceless still remain.
And so, upon his love intent,
Manly and nobly Richard went,
And to the haughty sire confessed
The hopes and fears which filled his breast.
Stern was Guy Allen's face, and bright
His dark eye shone with angry light;
And swiftly rising from his seat
He forward strode with rapid feet;
Then back again, as if inclined
With motion swift to ease his mind.
Thus back and forth his room he paced
Until he thrice its length had traced;
Till the composure, hard and cold,
Disturbed at first, returned three-fold.
Then in an icy tone he said,
While he held high his haughty head,
"I grant the service you have done
Our life-long gratitude has won;
And I would willingly repay
In every fair and worthy way,

With friendly help, or counsel true,
This debt so great and justly due.
Wherefore my words to you are weak ;
What I would say I dare not speak ;
And so the answer brief is best
And silence shall convey the rest,
Ask what you will of land or gold —
My daughter's hand I must withhold."

A pallor spread o'er Richard's face,
And yet he spoke with inborn grace,
Albeit with a warmth which proved
Beyond a doubt how much he loved :
" I make for service great or small
To you or yours no claim at all.
If, in the scope of God's design,
Some deed of duty has been mine,
I will not be so foolish, vain,
For this material aid to gain.
But, oh ! forgive me if I dare
Once more my heart's love to declare — "
" It is enough," Guy Allen said,
And darkly frowning, shook his head ;
" 'Tis true you have preserved her life,
But still she cannot be your wife."

" And why," the young man hotly cried,
" Is then to me this boon denied ?

Why must my hopes, so long deferred,
Again be in my heart interred,
Till, day by day and year by year,
Bereft of what I hold most dear,
Crowned with no joy, but filled with care,
My heart sinks into dull despair?
And is there nothing I can do
To prove how well I love, how true?
Oh, bid me strive, as Jacob strove,
Through the long years to gain his love,
And I will suffer and be strong
Through patient labor, dumb and long.
We are content with any lot
But that of parting — part us not;
For her true love goes out, dear sir,
To me, as mine goes out to her."

Now burned Guy Allen's anger more
Than it had ever flamed before,
No more discreet, but loud and wild,
His words burst forth : —
                    " Ungrateful child!
And has she dared my will to thwart —
To harbor treason in her heart?
And has she sent her willing slave
Her father's righteous ire to brave?

Know, then, bold youth, that if the day
Should come when you are wed with May,
Forever from this house she goes
And leaves me bitterest of her foes ;
My hatred shall her dowry be,
And I will curse the name of Leigh.
For I have sworn that if her line
Is tinged with baser blood than mine,
Henceforth to me she is no more
Than the vile beggar at my door."
With a red flush which proved how keen
This passionate, bitter thrust had been,
Richard arose and stood erect
In the full power of self-respect.
Manly he looked, and fair to see,
Clothed in unconscious dignity,
While his whole manner shadowed forth
His innate sense of noble worth.

" If you had held, proud sir, her charms
Too dear, too precious for my arms,
For any other cause, at will,
Than this, I would respect you still.
And though it left to others free
The precious love denied to me,
Out of that door, heart-filled with pain,
But silent, I had turned again.

But to declare your daughter's hand
Must better blood than mine command,
I say, New England's cities hold
In each true heart within their fold
A stream of life as pure, as fine,
As ever coursed through Allen's line;
And every soul that loves the right
Is just as good, in Heaven's sight,
Despite of birth, or name, or place,
As any son of Allen's race."

With anger Allen turned about.

"Nay," said Leigh, calmly, "hear me out.
Spare idle threats — for these I care
No more than for a breath of air.
And had I loved your daughter less,
And wished with her my suit to press,
Out of your house I would have borne
My love in spite of all your scorn.
But I would spare her future pain
At any cost of selfish gain.
I will not tempt her filial truth,
Old age shall not reproach her youth;
As she has been she still must be —
Her father's child — though loving me.
Forgive me, sir, if I have been
In word or temper far too keen;

For if you knew how sharp the smart
Which rankles deeply in my heart,
You would forgive, though every word
Had touched you like a two-edged sword.
Farewell!" and turning he was gone,
And the proud father stood alone.

RICHARD'S DEPARTURE.

WHAT passed that day between the two
The curious gossips never knew.
But wide the village oped its eyes,
Lost in conjecture and surprise,
And much it gaped and hard it gazed,
And oft its hands in wonder raised,
When busy tongues the rumor bore
That Leigh would practise there no more.
Vain were their questions, warm and kind,
To learn the secret of his mind;
Though ever courteous, kind and fair,
He would with none his secret share.
Except that in his darkened eye,
A settled sorrow seemed to lie,
Except that on his face the shade
Of sorrowing thought its impress laid,

And that his mien was strangely grave,
No other certain sign he gave.
And soon they heard him say " Farewell!"
But whither he went no man could tell.

MAY'S DECLINE.

MAY heard the news and from that hour.
She drooped as droops a fading flower;
Distress was written on her brow;
Her merry laugh had vanished now.
And thus the last of Allen's line
Sank into swift and sure decline.

Guy Allen, filled with pain and fear,
Seeing the shadow drawing near,
Of the dark angel, whose return
He sadly dreaded to discern,
Sought to discover if he might,
Some potent plan by which the light
Of joy and pleasure might retrace
Their happy smiles in May's dear face;
And with a desperate feeling sought
To rouse her from her gloomy thought.
But all his labor was in vain :
May would not — could not smile again.

At length in hope that other sights,
Strange scenes, new beauties, fresh delights,
Might from his daughter's heart remove
The cancer of her hopeless love,
Allen determined they should go
On journeys various to and fro,
Where balmy air and summer skies
Delight the sense and please the eyes ;
Till interest new and time should cure
The wound her heart could not endure.

SLEEP, MEMPHIS.

WHERE the broad river onward flows,
The southern twilight darker grows,
And, resting now on Memphis' breast,
Lulls her to sweet repose and rest.
A thousand lights yet brightly gleam,
Reflected in the placid stream.
While borne upon its spacious tide,
Colossal steamers onward glide,
Huge shadows on the river's breast
Like clouds that on the earth do rest,
Dark all, except that glowing line
Where lights through cabin windows shine,

And at the smoke-stack's towering heights
Are seen the colored signal lights.
In street and alley and green lane.
The evening bells are heard again,
While gently stealing on their way,
The evening breezes softly sway.
Go back ! go back ! oh, evening breeze !
The poison of a thousand trees,
Whose leaves are death, is in your touch,
And deadlier than a serpent's clutch,
And fiercer than a serpent's hiss
Is your caressing hold and kiss.
Sleep, Memphis, in your slumber deep ;
For this shall be your last sweet sleep
Ere toil and terror and distress
Drive out your peace and happiness.
Peace to the house where strangers dwell,
Silence and rest while all is well ;
Quiet oblivion watch her door
Who sleeps while yet her heart is sore ;
Who tosses on her pillow soft,
Lost in sad dreams and moaning oft,
Too weak her waking watch to keep,
Too sad to find refreshing sleep.
And peace to him whose light still **burns**
As fitfully he walks and turns

Within his room, or anxious marks,
As by his door, ajar, he harks,
Across the intervening hall,
The sad unconscious moans, which fall
From the pale lips, which once so gay,
Are fading silently away.
Sleep, stern old man! rest gently now
Ere deeper care-lines mark your brow ;
Sleep while you may — the time is nigh
When slumber from your couch shall fly,
And Allen's pride shall strive in vain
With anxious fear and burning pain.

THE HERO OF PEACE.

THE morning came, and with it fled
The peace of Memphis, for men said,
With blanchèd cheeks and quivering mouth,
" The pest is coming from the south ! "
Then eyes with tears began to fill,
And pallid cheeks grew paler still,
And turning to the safer north,
All who could journey issued forth.
The doctor stood within his door,
Where pleading friends were grouped before,

"The yellow curse no man can stay ;
Away from this valley of death, away !"
But the doctor sturdily shook his head,
And, gently answering, thus he said :
" Farewell, farewell to all my friends ;
But here my duty is -- and ends,
If God so wills. I cannot shirk
This plainly necessary work.
Little enough of help will be,
When few remain and many flee."
" But if you die !" his comrades cried.
" The Lord knows best ; let Him decide."

They left him as a man self-doomed,
But in their hearts, for his sake, bloomed
Flowers of love, whose fragrance rare,
'Twere highest earthly bliss to share.
For he who meets a human foe,
With force contending, blow for blow,
And on the field of battle falls,
Where patriotic duty calls,   •
Is less deserving of our praise
Than he who, in more quiet ways,
But in a pestilential breath
Which is the very air of death,
Goes forth to combat or endure
A foe more keen, a death more sure.

FACE TO FACE.

THE scourge came quickly to its prey :
Over the strong it held its sway ;
It scattered the young, gathered the old,
And held high carnival with the bold.
With deed of comfort, word of cheer,
Summons answering, far and near,
The doctor went his daily round ;
Where need was greatest he was found.
His smiling face, and cheery voice,
And wondrous skill, made men rejoice ;
And oft rekindled Hope's bright fire,
Which had just threatened to expire.
Once, as at evening's darkling close,
He sought a moment's sweet repose,
That on the morn he might repair
Into the fever-haunted air
With strength renewed, in haste there came
A messenger, who named a name
Whereat his very marrow thrilled
As if by sudden frost 'twere chilled ;
And up he sprang, and forth he went,
As one on earnest purpose bent,
Knowing that life depends, indeed,
Upon each moment's utmost speed.

Hot, parched, delirious, fever-sore,
Far from his dear New England shore,
Guy Allen tossing lay, with none
To comfort or attend, save one, —
His daughter May, whose pallid brow
Rivalled the valley lilies now ;
And who, in agony intense,
Born of her terrible suspense,
Silently wept, and watched, and prayed
That the Destroyer might be stayed.
At last, when hope was almost dead,
May Allen heard a hasty tread,
Which, drawing nearer, stopped before
The sick-room's partly-open door.
The doctor knocked. " Come in," she cried :
And then the door was opened wide.
And in that unexpected place,
Richard and May stood face to face.
A silent pressure of the hand,
A look which both could understand,
A few low words, which each let fall
In earnest greeting — this was all ;
Then, as by sudden impulse stirred,
They turned, without another word,
And to his need, who had suppressed
Their early hopes, their thought addressed.

THE HEART REBUKED.

'Twas a hard battle, but at length
Disease gave way to skill and strength,
And once more from his bed of pain
Guy Allen slowly rose again.
Arose to see death's shadow fall
On simple home and mansion hall ;
Even as when Egypt's fatal morn
Disclosed the doomed and slain first-born.
Or Rachel, o'er her lovely dead,
Refusing to be comforted.
To see distinction all give way
Before the danger of the day.
To see, where sickness and distress
Evoke that wondrous tenderness
Of human sympathy, all pride
Of every nature swept aside ;
To see, on every hand, how free
And universal love can be ;
To see the whole broad land outpour
Its generous aid at Memphis' door :
Arose to learn, with secret shame,
How empty is a noble name,
When all the callous heart has been
So wrapped its cloak of pride within ;

To feel the stern rebuke that worth
Ranks wealth, ranks pride, ranks noble birth.
And love is still, in every heart,
Above all else, its better part.
And now, as Allen stronger grew,
And in his eye the light anew
Witnessed to health's returning sway,
And ere they could his care repay
Or e'en had thanked him as they might,
The doctor vanished from their sight.
Then Allen, all subdued and changed,
Resolved they should not be estranged,
But, Richard found, he would recall
The angry words he had let fall.   .
He sought him then with intent kind,
But Leigh at home he could not find,
And, fearing to remain too long,
For May was neither well nor strong,
The travellers now their steps retraced,
And homeward sped, with prudent haste.

THE LAST VICTIM.

THE end for which the nation prayed
Had come ; the pestilence was stayed,
And hope revived, and commerce made
The streets resound with noise of trade ;

And daily fewer died — till none
Remained in danger more, save one.
That one, who had all danger dared,
And every toil and hardship shared ;
Who had remained when others fled
To help the sick and clothe the dead,
Now helpless lay, while in his frame
Burned the consuming fever's flame.
Men prayed, and gentle women wept,
As through the land the sad news swept,
And as it sped upon its way
It came to Allen and to May.

Then May's heart yearned for **Richard Leigh**,
And she cried out in agony ;
And her white arms were upward tossed ;
Yet, ere the cry its echo lost,
Even in the passing of the thought,
Her mind with brave resolve was fraught.
Then she sought Allen quickly, cried
Aloud she would not be denied.
" I cannot, will not. let him die
Alone — without a loved one nigh —
And he shall know my heart can hold
A love that never can grow cold.
Father, forbear the angry frown ;
Look on your child in pity down.

Oh! censure not; your stern behest
I hitherto have not transgressed;
But now my heart will surely break
If I my dying love forsake."

Then Allen took her hand, and said,
While a strange smile his face o'erspread,
"For his good deeds I would in truth
Some favor show this comely youth;
Wherefore, once more toward Memphis borne
I will go forth to-morrow morn;
But you, my daughter, must remain
And tarry till I come again.
Yet rest content. I promise you
What man can do, that I will do."
With a fair face so cheerily,
But, oh! at heart so wearily,
Sadder, indeed, than tongue can tell,
She kissed and bade her sire farewell.

THE JOYFUL RETURN.

MAY ALLEN by the window stood,
And looked abroad in pensive mood.
Broad and fair the acres lay
But she observed them not that day.

The sky was clear : but, deep in thought
May Allen saw, and marked it not.
The nimble rabbit through the wood
Darted in eager search of food ;
On trees and field May might have seen
Full twenty shades of brown and green ;
Far off a mountain-top lay bare
Environed by its icy air ;
Before, the unimpeded light
On distant village walls flashed bright ;
And just beyond, the broad blue sea,
Calm in its peaceful dignity,
As if upon its heaving breast
Ne'er rose the waters' foam-topped crest,
Lay still beneath the autumn sun,
While on the horizon, one by one,
The masts dipped down and out of sight,
Or slowly rose into the light.
But to this landscape beautiful
May Allen's eyes and sense were dull.
A letter on the window-sill
Lay open, read the lines who will.
" Richard is well again ; at length
He has regained his health and strength.
There is no more for me to do.
And I will now return to you."

No word from Richard, not the least
On which her longing eye might feast.
And so her fingers on the pane
Tapped to her heart's unsung refrain,
" He comes no more — he loves me not —
I am forgot — I am forgot."

Wrapped in these thoughts she does not see
A coach approaching speedily ;
In sad abstraction, never hears
The joyful sound of village cheers ;
Nor marks, as moodily she stands,
The signal of uplifted hands.
The servants hasten to and fro,
And wide the hall-door open throw ;
The dogs, in unrestrained glee,
Run wild and bark uproariously.
Full well they know, with instinct keen,
What these unusual sounds may mean,
And bay with all their might and main
To welcome Allen home again.

Still May before the window stood
Looking abroad in pensive mood,
When, suddenly, her name she heard,
Spoken with an endearing word.

Quick beat her heart — hot flamed her cheek
She started — turned — essayed to speak —
" Oh, Richard ! "   " Darling May," and then
The parted hands were joined again ;
And their eyes' lovelight told how much
Each heart thrilled at this happy touch.

CLOSING WORDS.

But little more have I to tell
Except to say that " all is well ! "
Even as the watch of old went by
And voiced his reassuring cry.
For, two months from that happy time,
The village bells began to chime ;
And ere the sun's declining ray
Had marked the closing hour of day,
Out of the dear old church at last,
Richard and May together passed
As man and wife, amid the cheers
Of the warm-hearted villagers.
And such a feast as then was spread
In Allen's mansion — so 'tis said —
Before or since has never been
Within that peaceful village seen.

And never from those joyous days
Was Allen proudly heard to praise
His name, or hold its claims above
The claims of honest worth and love ;
And much I fear that he may yet
Forget that old earl's coronet.

BETWEEN TIMES.

POETICAL SELECTIONS.

POETICAL SELECTIONS.

JAMES A. GARFIELD.

SEPTEMBER 19, 1881.

LAS! the bitter day is here,
The saddest day of all the year.
   A great man has been stricken down,
   A strong man has been overthrown,
   My chief, my president, my own,
Lies dead upon his bier.

We hear the solemn church-bells toll,
We hear the boom of cannon roll ;
   Our eyes are dimmed, we cannot rest,
   There is a burden on the breast,
   The world is weeping for its best,
Its most heroic soul.

It is a sadness all too deep
For words ; we can but weep and weep,
   And, weeping, deck the mournful land
   With sombre wreath and dark-hued band,
   Let every flag at half-mast hang,
And sorrowing vigils keep.

He was so noble and so good ;
Upright before the world he stood,
His life an open book, where light
On every page shone clear and white,
And every word was pure and bright,
　　Through varying time and mood.

The struggles of his youthful life,
His patience in that early strife,
His constant purpose, well and true
The right to teach, the right to do,
Into a sterling manhood grew,
　　A power with lessons rife.

Through all the change of place and power,
Through each temptation of the hour,
He held his way, nor turned aside
To fawn, to threaten, or deride ;
God and his country he allied ; —
　　This was his rock and tower.

Not less his sweet domestic shrine,
The graces of his modest line,
Not less his true devotion, shown
In every look, in every tone,
For those whose love was his alone
　　Shall make his glory shine.

The planet that at Mentor rose
Now as a star of glory glows,
Its lustre marked by every eye ;
It will not fade, it will not die.
Lo ! as the years to be go by,
 In beauty still it grows.

His life is o'er, his work is done ;
He sleeps, but in his sleep lives on.
For men can hear, and men can see,
And this the best, it seems to me,
Of all that men shall say, will be,
 " He made his people one."

THE CRY OF THE WHITE SLAVE.

AS I pondered in the gloom,
 Quiet as the silent tomb,
In the darkness and the weirdness that was
 gathered in my room,
 Through my nerves there crept a shiver,
 Colder than an icy stream,
 Making all my marrow quiver,
 And the place a horror seem,

Fearfully I bowed my head,
With a vague and nameless dread,
Like the signal and forewarning of the coming of
    the dead ;
        While, without, the rain was falling,
        And the thunder grated by,
        When a wraith, a shade appalling,
        Suddenly transfixed my eye.

Never shall my heart forget
What that night my room beset,
What congealed me into silence by a fear remem-
    bered yet.
        And the words, the words of burning,
        That the wraith, in solemn dole
        Uttered, ever are returning,
        They are written on my soul.

Bent his form, and slow his pace,
Coarse of feature, low of race,
While a look of awful sadness rested on his spirit-
    face.
        And I cried, in fear retreating,
        " Who art thou, oh, silent guest ?
        Where thy home, and wherefore fleeting
        From the silence of thy rest ? "

Suddenly a light then grew
Round the spectre, strange and new,

As if some unearthly lamp its ghostly light upon
    him threw.
        Half in fear and half in pity,
            Then I saw the shade was one
        Of the hundreds in the city
            Of the weary and unknown.

    Dust-begrimed and dirt-defiled,
    Wrinkle over wrinkle piled,
Wounded, ragged, hopeless, dreary, and by sorrow
    rendered wild,
        Stood the spectre that appalled me,
            And whose words, as weird they ran,
        In their vehemence appalled me,
            While it solemnly began :

    "Oh ! a song for some relief ;
    Oh ! a word to soothe our grief ;
Oh ! an act of simple justice to the lowly from the
    chief.
        From our dangers some protection,
            For our struggles some reward,
        Give, oh, give us some concession,
            For the work is very hard.

    " Often have our graves been made
    With the pickaxe and the spade,
Toiling where the weak foundation and the crum-
    bling walls are laid.

Oh, the crash, the falling shower
Of the heavy wood and stones !
Oh, the many wrecks that tower
Over crushed and broken bones !

"Fetch and carry, dig and toil,
In all weathers, freeze or broil ;
Oh, the veriest slaves are we of all the slaves above
the soil.
Come and breathe the poisonous gases
Of the sewers where we crawl ;
In the cellars, damp morasses,
Come and wonder why we fall.

"Still the hungry must be fed,
Still the weary round we tread,
Though the overtaxing labor brings the weary to
the dead.
Still in heated mills we smother,
Still we walk in crowded ways,
Jostling one against the other
In the monotone of days."

Thus it spoke, and said no more,
And it vanished from the floor,
Gliding, fading into darkness through the partly-
open door.
But an echo, softly calling,
All my being strangely thrilled,

And the silence round me falling
With unspoken speech was filled.

Up I sprang, and outward sped
To the darkness, while I said,
Stretching forth my hands imploring to the spirit
who had fled,
" Let me — let me not be taunted
By the memory of thy gloom !
Let me — let me not be haunted
By thy presence in my room ! "

And the shade has ne'er returned,
But the words that I have learned
Deep within my heart are printed, and into my
heart are burned.
And subdued is every pleasure,
As, long haunted by its lay,
Still I hear the doleful measure
Of the voice that seems to say,

"Oh, for one to right the wrong !
Oh, for some one rich and strong,
Who will set the drift of doing to the current of
my song ;
Who will make the burdens lighter,
That the workers have to bear,
Who will make the daylight brighter
To the toilers everywhere."

GILBERT RAY.

THROUGH the burning thirst for gold,
Sadly to dishonor sold,
One, exalted in men's eyes,
Blindly trusted, falls and flies.

Gilbert Ray has staked and lost,
Reckless of what it might cost,
In his keen desire for wealth,
Funds that were not his, by stealth.

Day by day, from sin to sin,
Gilbert Ray went deeper in,
Till, in one stupendous theft,
Friend and patron were bereft.

Nothing sacred in his sight;
Orphan's fortune, widow's mite,
Poor man's saving, or the loan
Made in friendship — all are gone.

On a bubble, which has burst,
He had staked his money first;
Then of others, failed, and fled,
And his fair, fair fame is dead.

Would I change with Gilbert Ray
For the wealth of Indies ? Nay !
Than this man the meanest poor,
Be he honest, is worth more.

Gilbert Ray, the deeds you wrought
Shall be scorpions to your thought,
Memory's lash shall never cease
To disturb your rest and peace.

Gilbert Ray, your once proud name
Is to-day a sound of shame.
Children's children, yet unborn,
Shall remember you with scorn,

Spite of long delay of law,
Spite of legal trick and flaw,
This your sure reward shall be,
Punishment and misery.

Breach of trust ! I do not care
By what gentle name you bear
Your rash guilt ; the truth is brief,
He who steals is but a thief.

Hush ! I will not have it said
One who takes a loaf of bread
Earns, alas ! a harsher name
Than the robber, steeped in shame.

On my soul the truth is pressed,
Honest living still is best ;
Sterling hearts rank fortunes great,
Character is more than state.

Gilbert Ray, I bid you pray
For forgiveness to-day ;
Humbly now that mercy crave
Which you need beyond the grave.

Be not callous, but repent ;
Prove that you are penitent ;
As you wronged men, now be true,
And return to them their due.

LITTLE BENNIE.—LITTLE MAMIE.

SHALL I tell you of the stream
    Where a little boy once played,
Where the moon its silver beam
    Touched upon a blue-eyed maid ?
        It is not a tale of wonder,
            Though it happened long ago ?
        It will rend no veil asunder ;
            Shall I tell it ?   Be it so.

Little Bennie, child of eight,
    Little Mamie, child of three ;
Happy children, hearts elate
    With their young life's joy and glee.
Hand in hand, they wander gaily
    Through the meadows, rich and green ;
Picking flowers, finding daily
    Beauties that they ne'er had seen.

Little Bennie, child of ten,
    Little Mamie, child of five ;
Hero small and heroine,
    When in school they bravely strive
Down to keep that dreadful feeling,
    With the pedagogue in view,
Which is in their hearts revealing
    Timid fears they never knew.

Youthful Bennie, boy fifteen,
    Little Mamie, girl of ten ;
Lurking glances, scarcely seen,
    Painful blushes mounting when
Schoolboys, hiding by the river,
    See them hand in hand depart,
Shouting when they see him give her
    Candy-kiss and sugar-heart.

Ben, the student, twenty-one,
　　Schoolgirl Mamie, sweet sixteen ;
Strolling where the ripples run,
　　In the moonlight's silver sheen ;
By the olden river, tresses
　　Lightly on a shoulder laid ;
By the dear old river, kisses
　　True for lover and for maid.

Ben, just turning twenty-eight,
　　Mamie, flower of twenty-three ;
Both a trifle proud of late,
　　For a boy is on her knee.
Little hero, boldly crowing,
　　Dancing on his mother's arm,
Little heeding, little knowing
　　Of the mother's love so warm.

Ben, just forty, thoughtful brow,
　　Mary, thirty-five, dear wife ;
Study bringing care-lines now
　　With the earnestness of life.
Steady gait and sober talk,
　　Charity more deep, more broad,
Striving in the path to walk
　　That leads upward unto God.

Ben, a man of fifty-five,
   Mary, fifty, turning gray ;
Home, sweet home, a perfect hive —
   Children, taller e'en than they.
And Love's holy light still shining
   On the hearth of many years,
Sheds a glory intertwining
   Faith and Hope with joy and tears.

Ben, gray, bent, and seventy-three,
   Mary, feeble, sixty-eight ;
Nearing their eternity,
   Trembling form and faltering gait.
Almost near the shining portal,
   Almost where the waters meet,
Almost with the waves immortal,
   Washing earth's dust from their feet.

Ben, a marble shaft stands high,
   With his name and " seventy-four ; "
Mary, "sixty-nine," hard by,
   Sleeps beside her love of yore,
By the olden river sleeping ;
   Dear old stream, which ne'er will tell
All the secrets in its keeping,
   Of the hearts that loved so well.

Thus have I, in simple wise,
    Told the simple tale I knew,
Not in wonder's strange disguise,
    But in story plain and true;
And the watchful, dear old river
    Murmurs softly o'er and o'er,
" Little Bennie lives forever,
    Little Mamie dies no more."

THE SLEEP OF THE LITTLE ONES.

NIGHT opens her mantle,
    Her flag is unfurled,
And darkness comes creeping
    All over the world.
Now into their cradles,
    Their cribs and their beds,
The little ones nestle
    Unnumbered wee heads.
The rose flush of health
    In their round faces shines,
No heartache to sorrow
    Their slumber confines.

Their prayers have been spoken,
   Each low-uttered word,
Who doubts that the Father
   Their whisper has heard?
Ah yes, for the faith
   That is strong in all prayers
To move even mountains,
   If need be, is theirs.
Their trusting prayer ended
   They kiss us "good night;"
The eyes gently closing
   Are lost to the light.
Each round little head,
   On its soft pillow pressed,
Lies there oblivious,
   Serenely at rest.
And lo! in a moment
   Their thoughts fly away,
To realms of rare beauty
   Where we may not stray,
Each little mind busy
   With wonders and toys,
A world of weird happiness,
   Gaily enjoys.
And so, safely passing
   The dark hours through,

They sleep till the morning
Awakes them anew.
Oh blessed, thrice blessed,
The homes where they sleep,
And long may each circle
Its little ones keep ;
For truly the world
Has no blessing like this —
A child's faithful love
And a child's loving kiss.
Then sleep, gentle darlings,
While God's mighty arm
And His holy angels
Protect you from harm.

THE DEATH OF FAITHFUL ROVER.

IIE children are dreary and sad to-day,
And some of them are crying ;
Their little long faces are wet with tears,
For Rover — Old Rover — is dying.
They call him pet names and stroke his long hair ;
They whistle and chirrup together ;
But the kind old playmate is with them there
For the last, last time forever.

He opens a moment his wistful eyes ;
  They see it, and call him, " Rover ; "
A faint, low whine, and he tries to rise,
  And then — poor fellow — it's over.
And never again through the tangled wood,
  The bees and wild birds chasing,
Shall the old dog scatter the partridge brood,
  Or bound with the children racing.

They call him again, again and again,
  They raise his head and shake him ;
Their little hearts break, but all in vain ;
  They never more shall wake him.
No more through the copse and the underbrush
  Shall he leap, the hare pursuing ;
No more will he bark at the tender thrush,
  Or bay when the storm is brewing.

They will miss the old dog, with his honest face,
  And his tail so briskly wagging,
And the summer days will have lost their grace,
  And their daily plays go lagging.
They will miss him, away from the old house-door.
  And the yard will look drear without him ;
And those merriest days will come no more
  When the children were all about him.

When, patient and plodding, he bore them all,
  With never a growl of warning ;
And trod so gently that none might fall,
  And guarded them night and morning ;
And when the little ones sank to rest,
  Asleep on the grass and clover,   .
They nestled their heads on the shaggy breast
  Of faithful, dear old Rover.

And so the children are dreary and sad,
  And all of them now are crying ;
Their little long faces are wet with tears
  Where Rover — old Rover — is lying.
They make him a grave in the hillside fair,
  Where they may forget him never ;
Then cover him gently and leave him there
  In his peaceful rest forever.

THE SOUTHERN WIND.

THE wind blows east—the wind blows north—
   The wind blows west — I care not ;
But, oh ! the wind that's from the south
   I love to greet but dare not.
Fair, fair those southern breezes are,
   Soft are their sweet caresses ;
Alas ! their music from afar
   My heavy heart distresses.

Oh, Lilian, thou wert pure and fair,
   Sweet, gentle southern daughter,
As oft we wandered free from care
   Beside yon rippling water.
And still that water ripples on
   Beneath the moon's fair splendor ;
But, Lilian, Lilian, thou art gone —
   Oh, Lilian, true and tender !

The cypress marks thy early tomb ;
   Too soon its dark green foliage
Is mingled with the scented bloom
   Of thy beloved magnolias.

And flowers grow and flowers fade
  Where thou, fair Lilian, sleepest ;
But, oh, of all the flowers thus laid,
  Thou wert, dear love, the sweetest.

Oh, Lilian, Lilian, dark indeed
  The days will be without thee.
My heart is sad, for memory clings
  In broken love about thee.
The breeze so soft, thy rosy cheeks
  To darker roses turning,
Has now a sadder touch, and speaks
  Of unavailing yearning.

The valley of the river turns
  Unto a beauty olden ;
The bosom of the river burns
  With splendor rich and golden.
And slowly through the orange grove,
  With all its sweet delaying,
The gentle southern breeze, oh, love !
  Is softly toward me straying.

The wind blows east—the wind blows north—
  The wind blows west — I care not ;
But, oh, the wind that's from the south
  I love to greet and dare not.

For flowers grow and flowers fade
　Where thou, lost Lilian, sleepest ;
But, oh, of all the flowers thus laid,
　Thou wert, dear love, the sweetest.

THE BATTLE OF THE CLOUDS.

HE clouds in the air are at battle ;
　The white are marshalled against the black,
　The black are marching against the white ;
While over them both the sky is blue,
And under them both my heart is true.
But whether it be
　　　　That she, to me,
Is true as my heart, so let it be
　That hope shall strive for the white ;
　Despair for the black shall fight ;
Now lightning cleave and thunder rattle,
And let the wild wind judge the battle.

How still the earth is under :
Lazily shines the evening sun,
The flowers fall nodding, one by one.

The shadows are long of the old oak trees,
And motionless under the still green leaves,
For even the breeze
        From under the trees,
Has gone to the war, and left the bees
To drowsily hum and sail at ease;
But all is changed in frightened wonder,
Since gleams the lightning, roars the thunder.

Who of the two shall master? —
Gabriel leads in the van of the white,
Lucifer rides on the brow of the black.
Lucifer's forces are dark and strong,
And low in the heavens they roll along;
While up in the sky,
        So very high —
It makes me dizzy to see them fly —
Gabriel's lifeguard is hurrying by.
   They poise a moment and then they dash;
   There is a gleam and a dismal crash!
Faster the north wind sweeps, and faster!
The firmament rocks in the dread disaster —
And fearful and trembling I wait the master.

Be still, my heart, and faint not!
The battle is hot in the vaulted dome;
Over the earth does a darkness come.

Now Gabriel's lightning pierces through
Lucifer's left and shows the blue ;
While on the right,
        The forces of night
Thunder against the army of light ;
And wilder and wilder the wind sweeps down,
And fiercer and fiercer the strife goes on,
And darker and darker the black clouds come.
  Be brave, my soul, and shrink not !
  Be still, my heart, and faint not !

Ah ! struggles my hope in the sunlight ?
Gleams Gabriel's lightning on Lucifer's brow,
The thunderbolt falls on the earth below,
And the hosts of Lucifer, pierced and slain,
Dash to the earth in torrents of rain.
Ah ! joy is me.
       It now must be
That she is as true as my heart ; for see !
As an arch of triumph above the goal
Of the victor — a rainbow from pole to pole.
Glories on glories the skies unfold,
Streaked by the sun into purple and gold.
Ah ! sweet is the voice of my love to-day,
  And my song is a song of thanksgiving,
  For I live in the faith of believing ;
That the love that was glad in the sunlight

Shall entwine and protect in the twilight;
That the heart that was true in the shadowy fight,
Shall be strong and endure through the darkness of
    night.

DAYS OF YORE.

AN oak tree by my window,
    An elm tree by the door,
    Through which the moonlight streaming
      Throws shadows as of yore;
    Dark leaf sprites! ghostly do ye dance,
      Weird shapes upon my floor!

Except where the moon is shining,
    The room is dark and dim;
And it seems to me — though it still may be
    A fancy, a dream, a whim —
That the shadows are darker to-night than e'er,
    Darker and still more grim.

A friend with light comes near me,
    Oh, pitying friend, depart!
Nor light, nor friends, nor merry cheer
    Nor melody, nor art,

Would drive the gloom of this darkened room
  Out of my heart of hearts.

Oh, moonlight, soft and tender!
  Oh, leaflets green and true!
You make my heart remember
  A face I saw with you,
A vision as pure as the stars that shine
  In heaven's unchanging blue.·

Beneath yon elm tree straying,
  On such a night as this,
With all Love's sweet delaying,
  And all Love's happiness,
We gathered an age of paradise
  In a single evening's bliss.

But darkly and at midnight
  The spirit of Death came on,
And she heard him, and ere daylight
  She followed and was gone,
While sorrowing winds came through the trees
  In a sad and desolate moan.

Still mild and softly streaming,
  The moonlight floods the earth,
Each house is roofed with silver,
  All have a sweet new birth,

And here with me the shadows cling
  About my lonely hearth.

Oh, is there no returning
  Of dear ones torn away ?
Can it be true that man is naught
  But perishable clay ?
No, no ! for I will meet my love
  Somewhere, somehow, some day.

Come, Night, with all your shadows,
  Come, Shades, with all your gloom,
Oh, sombre throng, come quickly,
  Fill up my empty room,
For here your dark dominion ends,
  You cannot pass the tomb.

Then back, dark thoughts, and perish !
  Back to your haunts, and die !
The love that still I cherish
  Shall bring the loved one nigh ;
And all night's shadows shall not hide
  The love-glance of her eye.

MARGY BROWN.

ARGY BROWN! Margy Brown!
Cease, I pray, your wondrous smiling ;
There is something so beguiling
In your smile, that I am whiling
    All my precious time away,
    And I must not, cannot stay ;
For the sun is slowly setting,
And the sky is darker getting,
While my soul is fretting, fretting,
    And it seemeth to declare,
    Beware of Margy Brown! Beware!

Margy Brown! Margy Brown?
Do not touch me with your finger
Do not let it gently linger
In my hand, and do not hinder
    Thus my going ; let me go.
    Mischief! can I leave you so ?
See, the daylight now is dying,
And the shadows thick are lying
Underneath the elm tree, vying
    With the shade of your dark hair.
    Beware, oh, Margy Brown! Beware!

Margy Brown! Margy Brown!
See you not the darkness crawling?
Hear you not a soft voice falling?
Hark! it is my mother calling,
   Calling for her laggard son ;
   Send me from you, pretty one :
Turn away that brown eye shining,
That is in my soul entwining,
Undefined and undefining,
   Love-thoughts that I must not share ;
   Beware, sweet Margy Brown! Beware!

Margy Brown! Margy Brown!
Who is he who lingers yonder?
On what mission does he ponder?
When I part from you I wonder,
   Margy, will he come to you?
   Does he love you, Margy, too?
Sweetheart, it was only jesting,
That my haste from you was pressing ;
I will stay, my love confessing,
   While my heart, it says, Beware!
   Some one sees that she is fair —
Take care of Margy Brown! take care!

CHARLES SUMNER.

Written for the St. Louis " Globe," shortly after the death of Hon. CHARLES SUMNER.

OLUMBIA'S halls are desolate,
　　Dark shadows in her chambers brood :
With blinding tears she mourns the fate
　　Of him, the gifted and the good.
She kneels, in her impassioned woe,
　　Her arms enfold her voiceless son ;
She cannot, will not, let him go,
　　Although the battle has been won.
Crape flutters in the shuddering wind,
　　And sadly beats the muffled drum,
And lo ! before, around, behind,
　　To weep Columbia's children come.
Swift at his bier the tears descend,
　　And like the moaning of the sea
A million voices mourn the friend —
　　The noble friend — of Liberty.
Arise, Columbia ! do not weep ;
　　And ye, the children of her womb,
Behold, the soul of Sumner sleeps !
　　It will not moulder in the tomb.
Arise ! and let your praise be heard
　　That as he lived the patriot died ;

That, of the host of spoken words,
  God, Truth, and Freedom were his pride.
No sect controlled his grand design ;
  No boundary made his labor cease ;
Peace was the daystar of his mind, —
  In every land and nation — Peace !
Then let us deck our hero well
  With flowers ; in tears let smiles be seen ;
With garlands wind the tolling bell,
  And leave the sleeper in his dream.
Great warrior of peace, sleep on ! .
  Thy warfare has been bravely won ;
Thou art forever graved upon
  Our hearts, "Columbia's noble son."
Thy kind hands crossed upon thy breast,
  We dumbly honor while we kiss ;
We love thee in thy perfect rest,
  The statesman's highest honor this.
Sleep, then ; thy last undying speech
  And " I am tired," shall be heard
Till land to sister land shall reach,
  With common impulse stirred.
God give us peace ! and when the voice
  Of anger cries for war and woe,
Let us remember Sumner's choice,
  And, like bold freemen, answer " No !"

THE ASHMAN.

ITH bell-like voice and cadence strong,
  A trail of dust around him falling.
The ashman quaintly chants the song
  Which heralds his approach and calling.

His creaking wagon, bony steed
  And ragged clothes match well together ;
A certain index of the need
  That makes him cry, though rough the weather,
    " Haul yo' ashes !   Haul yo' ashes !
    Dirt an' ashes — do yo' haulin' !"

However, on his coal-black face
  There is no shadow of repining ;
The humblest of his patient race,
  His eye with calm content is shining.

I honor him because I know
  That he is cheerful and light-hearted,
Although through wind and rain and snow
  His dusty load is often carted.

What though the dust upon his hair
  And torn attire betray his station ?
While still upon the frosty air
  His voice rings like an inspiration,

" Haul yo' ashes !   Dirt an' ashes !
Now's de time to do yo' haulin' ! "

None would exchange their happier lot
    For his unenviable labor,
And yet, I warrant, there is not
    A truer friend or better neighbor.

For never from his open door
    Have homeless wanderers been driven,
And from his ever scanty store
    The generous gift is freely given,

And though he is of humble birth,
    And thoughtless youngsters oft deride him,
In all that makes up noble worth
    The town has few who stand beside him.

Shout on, old ashman !   Send your cries
    Through streets and alleys gaily ringing ;
Still preach contentment — patient, wise,
    And shame regret — while bravely singing
        " Haul yo' ashes !   Haul yo' ashes !
        Now's de time to do yo' haulin' !
        Dirt an' ashes, h'yur me callin',
        Haul yo' ashes !   Haul yo' ashes ! "

MY WIFE.

Y wife sits beside me —
Now who shall deride me?
Ho! who shall make merry when lovers are
wise?
Fall snow e'er so lightly,
Shine sun e'er so brightly,
They dull not, they dim not, the light of her eyes.

Wild leaping and lashing,
Mad on the rocks dashing,
Growl, old ocean hoary, with head of white foam;
Come crunching, come tearing,
Go back, all despairing,
I laugh and defy you, for I am at home.

Her hand my hand pressing
Gives back soft caressing;
Her voice, ever gentle, is loving and kind.
As daily she meets me
With glad smiles she greets me,
So happiness leads me and care lags behind.

Go, sot, to your bottle,
For soon it will throttle
The pitiful pleasure you find in despair ;
For all of your pleasure
Is not worth the measure
Of one waving strand of my wife's flowing hair.

You soon will grow weary,
But we shall be cheery.
When you are forgotten our song shall be heard.
Two hearts, but one-hearted,
Apart, yet not parted,
We journey along in the light of the Word.

We jog on together
Through rough and fair weather,
And each holds the other so neither shall fall ;
With kind words of soothing,
Life's rough places smoothing,
While sadness goes begging and sinks to the wall.

Then fall, snow, so lightly,
Blow, hollow winds, nightly,
Dash, surf of the sea, on the rocks thy white foam ;
The tempest may charm us
But never shall harm us,
For enter you cannot the circle of Home.

THE UNFORTUNATE SHOEMAKER.

IF you please, sir, could you tell, sir,
Whereabouts is Mr. Well's, sir?
Him as lives by making shoes, sir,
Some one said as how you knew, sir.

Do I know, boy? Yes, I do, boy,
Which is why I tell to you, boy,
It's a sad tale you must hear, boy,
He is near his last, I fear, boy.

If you please, sir, what's his ill, sir?
For it makes me rather chill, sir,
For to hear as how you tell, sir,
Mister Well, sir, isn't well, sir.

Listen, then, boy, you're his friend, boy,
Mr. Well has found his end, boy,
Waxed it was and in his sole, boy,
It did make a grievous hole, boy.

Whereupon when I did call, boy,
I found he had lost his awl, boy,
And I have no doubt he pegs, boy,
Even now on his last legs, boy.

If you please, sir, I'm askeered, sir,
And I'm very much afeared, sir,
How as which as Mr. Well, sir,
Never will be werry well, sir.

MY FEET ARE ON THE MOUNTAINS.

I.

M Y feet are on the mountains, but I cannot
see my way,
There is darkness all about me, for the
mist obscures the day,
But I know the sun is shining, though I cannot see
it now,
And I soon shall reach the summit of the moun-
tain's distant brow.
Then be lifted, O my heart of hearts, be joyful, O
my soul !
Let the waves of thankful gladness o'er my grate-
ful spirit roll ;
Send thy praise unto the Father, send thy love
unto the Son,
And thy reverence and homage to the sacred Holy
One.

II.

The path is steep and rugged, and the air is keen
and cold,

And the whirlwind and the tempest do my trembling limbs enfold,

And the thunder shakes the mountain, while the
lightning blinds my eye,

But the Lord of lords upholds me, and He will
not let me die.

Then be lifted, O my heart of hearts! Be joyful,
O my soul!

Let the waves of thankful gladness o'er my grateful spirit roll;

Lo! my praise is to the Father; lo! my love is to
the Son,

And my reverence and homage to the sacred Holy
One.

III.

The wild beasts of the mountains are the shadows
of my path,

I can hear their stealthy footfalls and the snarling
of their wrath;

They are near me and around me, and they seek
me to devour,

But the God of Daniel's lions is my refuge and my
power.

Then be lifted, O my heart of hearts! Be joyful,
 O my soul!
Let the waves of thankful gladness o'er my grate-
 ful spirit roll.
I will praise thy name, O Father! I will love thy
 name, O Son!
And my heart shall be thy temple, O thou sacred
 Holy One.

IV.

Lo! my eyes behold the light of day; I see my
 journey's end;
And I see the smile of beauty of the sinner's gra-
 cious Friend.
And the tempests and the wild beasts rage in im-
 potence below,
For the peace of God forever rests upon the
 mountain's brow.
Then be lifted, O my heart of hearts! Be joyful,
 O my soul!
Let the waves of thankful gladness o'er my grate-
 ful spirit roll.
Hallowed be thy name, O Father! Blessed be thy
 name, O Son!
Praise and love and adoration to the holy Three in
 One.

FACE THE MUSIC.

ACE the music, though the world should
   Turn against you in its might ;
Waver not, be not a coward,
   Dare to think and do what's right.

If reverses come, and sorrow
   Overtakes you on your way,
Face the music, and the morrow
   Will dawn brighter than to-day.

When a storm is breaking o'er you,
   Or an avalanche sweeps down,
And your life seems dark before you,
   And the world appears to frown,

And all friends prove false and leave you,
   E'en the friends you most do love,
And your fondest hopes deceive you,
   Face the music — look above.

Face the music, though the rattle
   Of the conflict jar your soul ;
Boldly enter Life's long battle,
   God your guide and **Heaven** your goal.

Face the music in Life's morning,
    Face it in the noontime bright ;
Face it in the twilight gloaming,
    Face it in the solemn night.

At all times and in all seasons,
    Wheresoever you may be,
Let no fear nor favor bind you,
    Face the music and be free.

MAXIMS.

EEK daily that which daily needs thy care.
    Think nothing fair which thou canst make
        more fair.
Give unto those who of thy bounty crave.
Desire to live, but do not fear the grave.
In all thou doest, all thy motives scan.
Love man, love God ; but love God more than man.
Be proud to know ; in knowing, be not proud.
Answer not anger with like anger loud.
As thou art human, all things human learn ;
As born for heaven, to things immortal turn.
Hold not opinion with too firm a grasp.
Thy heart and soul to faith and mercy clasp.

Curse not the erring, but compassion show.
Shun all the wrong, and do not give the blow.
Be free to laugh ; in laughter be not free,
But let thy mirth discretion-tempered be.
Sneer not at sports which make the body strong ;
Abstain from sports irreverent or wrong.
The jeering skeptic do not fear to face ;
But scoffers gather where shall come disgrace.
On slippery ground is he who stands on ice.
"Eat, drink, be merry," is a fool's device.
Claim not, however sure, the race as won
Till thou art victor and the race is done.
If thou hast done a good deed unto men,
Boast not of it, but do good deeds again.
If ruler, just ; if ruled, obedient be.
Honor thy word, and men shall honor thee.
And over all, where'er thou art proclaim
The free salvation in Immanuel's name.

FEAR NOT, DEAR HEART.

FEAR not, dear heart, though fashion brings
    Its changing fancies ever ;
The nearest and the dearest things
    Remain the same forever.

The ribbon may be red or blue,
　The glove be brown or yellow,
If but the owner's hand be true,
　The heart be warm and mellow.

Although the garment speaks the plan
　Of fashion's skilful planner,
The coat has never made the man
　Or custom made the manner.

What matters though my friend has sent
　His letter plain or tinted,
So that the words are frankly meant,
　Outspoken and unstinted.

For fashion cannot go beyond
　The range of human feeling;
A higher and a nobler bond
　Life ever is revealing.

A mother's unrepining love,
　A wife who never falters,
A faith in future life above,
　These, fashion never alters.

It cannot make the rivers flee
　Back to their early fountains,
Nor rule the tides, nor change for me　.
　The everlasting mountains.

It cannot kill the love of right,
   Nor quench the patriot fire,
Nor dash to earth with all its might
   The brave hearts that aspire.

It cannot stop the genial sun
   From shining on the flowers,
Nor keep the dew from resting on
   The grass in morning hours.

It cannot check the worlds that move
   Upon their paths diurnal,
Nor scorn the power and holy love
   Of God, the Lord Eternal.

And, oh! how does the tender spell
   Of Christ's love and compassion
In its simplicity repel
   All silly pride and fashion.

Then sorrow not, though fashion brings
   Its changing fancies ever;
Remember that the dearest things
   Remain the same forever.

UNCERTAINTY.

THROUGH what nervous fluctuations
And what painful palpitations,
Through what stages and gradations
    Of uncertain hope we pass.
Up to-day and down to-morrow,
Heights of joy and depths of sorrow,
Now we lend and now we borrow,
    Swaying like the summer grass.

II.

In one moment all elated,
With some golden plan inflated,
Till the brilliant bubble, freighted
    With a day-dream breaks and dies.
But the essence of that dreaming
Lingers, as a perfume seeming,
Balm like healing, and redeeming
    From despair, discouraged lives.

III.

In our changeable condition,
Failure comes, so does fruition ;
Both have their peculiar mission ;
    Hopes and doubts go hand in hand.

For we build our hopes resplendent
On a dozen things contingent,
Which themselves are but dependent
 On an *if* or on an *and*.

IV.

And 'tis well: the Father, knowing
What is best in His bestowing
For his children's safe upgrowing,
 Lets us struggle on our way;
Till we learn that disappointment
Is not evil, but an ointment
Of good will, of His appointment,
 Strengthening us from day to day.

WHEN I WOULD DIE.

 WOULD not die in childhood,
 When life's sweet buds have only just begun
 To greet the rising of the morning sun;
When every voice is only raised to bless,
And every gentle touch is a caress;
When whispered words are undisguised and sweet,
And human angels guard my baby feet;

When, tired of play, upon my mother's knee
I sleep, soothed by her tender lullaby ;
When in my springtime's overflowing cup
The holy debt of childhood is heaped up,
And mystery enfolds both earth and sky,
What need have I to die ?

No, let me rather live
In thankful, glad return my love to give
To those who loved me then ; in whose kind care
My feeble limbs grew strong.   I would repay
With tenfold blessings every blessing they
Strewed on my rosy path.   And gratefully
I would recall my mother's lullaby,
And, with her guidance, in the path of truth
I would press on to youth.

I would not die in youth.
When, in their matchless and their perfect bloom,
Life's opening flowers shed forth their sweet per-
fume ;
When the swift blood goes leaping through my
veins,
And yet my youthful memory retains
My mother's prayers.   When every hope is bright,
When the young heart is faithful to the right,
And sweeter beauties mark each changing sight ;

When, like a soldier fresh into the war,
Unharmed by hardship and unmarred by scar,
With eager haste I step into the strife
Upon the ancient battle-field of life,
When love is pure and earnest purpose high,
Why should I die?

No. Let me rather stay—
In truth and honor wend my youthful way,
Gird up my loins, set towards the mark my face,
And bravely entering Life's uncertain race,
Let me press on, while every healthful sign
Defies the blight of premature decline;
Let me press on, in youth's resistless might,
With wrong contending, and defending right.
So in the sure and steady course of time
I would reach manhood and attain my prime.

I would not die in manhood,
When the ripe fruit is hanging on the bough,
And the broad harvest is all whitened now;
When the clear vision of my later hour
Marks the full beauty of the open flower;
When the long race is very nearly run,
And the fierce battle has been almost won:
When the poor need me; when with word or deed
I may give comfort to the hearts that bleed;

When I may stand even as the oak in strength,
And tower amidst the storm, and when at length
I reach the summit of Life's mountain high,
　　What cause have I to die?

　　No.　Let me rather stand,
While manhood's power still moves my hardy hand,
A friend to all who need a faithful friend,
True to my trust, till from the time-worn stage
Of life I pass, in honored gray old age.

　　Then let me die.
When I am old, and there are none to love —
When all that I hold dear have passed above
The wrangle and the jar — when the plucked field
Of life is empty, and will no more yield
To me its store of sweets ; when I have run
The course God gave me, and my feeble sun
Is sinking fast to rest ; when I can say
That I have faithfully pursued my way,
Have done my duty ; when the last loved **head**
Lies underneath the faded flowers, dead,
Then I am ready.
　　　　　　　In what I have failed,
When I have faltered, proven false, or quailed,
I rest my cause with Him, who will forgive
For His Son's sake who died that I might live.
And so, contented, with no tears to weep,
With smiles, I will lie down, at last to sleep.

THE LESSON OF THE LEAVES.

S the leaves which now are dying,
 As the leaves which now are lying
 Browned and goldened in the fashion
 Of the olden autumn time ;
As the rich gloss on them streaming,
Or the frost upon them gleaming,
So Life's autumn tints soon coming
 On my heart will beam and shine.

As the leaves that glide and flutter
Downward, downward to the gutter,
Shrivelled, crisp, and brittle, rustling
 Ever in the same old way,
Thou, my cherished one, must alter,
Cool thine ardor, waver, falter,
In the time to come, returning
 To the Undiscovered Day.

And the old leaves — who can find them ?
Lo ! they leave no trace behind them :
Wind-blown, buried by a myriad
 Other leaves, they are no more.
So, my heart, thy short life's pleasure
Is but measured with the measure

Of a moment, and thou goest
   To a vast and unknown shore.

Then be true, dear heart, and ponder ;
Then be still, my heart, and wonder
What the faded leaves may teach thee,
   As they scatter to the ground.
Hark ! their voices, calling, calling,
Still, though ever falling, falling,
Breathing out their tender lesson
   With a clear and certain sound :

" Welcome, wind, that bears us onward ;
Welcome, wind, that beats us downward ;
We are floating, we are floating,
   To the place of rest we come ;
To our parent earth forever,
Lo ! we journey altogether ;
Root and tree and branch shall never
   Part us from our cherished home."

So then, heart of mine, remember,
In this chilling, drear November,
Even, as the dry leaves loosen,
   While the wind sweeps to and fro,
As the hour that long has sought them,
As the time that now has brought them,
Autumn, so to thee will autumn
   Come. Then be thou glad to go.

THE CREED OF LOVE.

HOWEVER low and wretched one may be,
   That which is noblest may survive the
   rest ;
Though full of evils, and perverted, he,
   If kindly sought, will answer to the quest.

Who that is fallen but sometimes does feel
   The spark of that almost extinguished fire
Which, through the vilest sin, does still reveal
   The life of secret hope and pure desire ?

Oh, do not say that it is now too late
   To save a single ruined life on earth.
The Master only is the arbiter of fate,
   And He decides what every soul is worth.

Still follow them with kindly deed and care
   Who are descending sadly to the deep :
The ready sympathy and earnest prayer
   May save them yet before their fatal leap.

How can we know, we, guarded by the ties
   Which home and love and friendship round us
      weave,

How in their hearts the solemn yearning lies,
   Their sins to spurn, their evil paths to leave?

Be ever ready, then, not to condemn,
   But to befriend them, and with glad surprise
They, too, will learn the evil to contemn
   Which is so despicable in our eyes.

Befriend them, that they too may issue forth,
   Still doing good out of pure heart and mind,
And it shall be, through blessing men on earth,
   Thou shalt receive the love of all mankind.

TURN ABOUT.

TURN about — turn about —
   This is fair play ;
Give every man a chance,
   That is the way.
Poor man to president,
Rover or resident,
All who are diligent
   Must have their day.

Turn about — turn about —
Fortune is fair ;
In this world bountiful
All have a share.
Every community
Has opportunity
For those who prudently
Work, and take care.

Turn about — turn about —
When you are wrong :
Better be right and true
Than be too strong.
Yield, but not wastefully ;
Gently and tastefully :
Giving way gracefully
Helps one along.

Life has its store for all,
Peasant and king ;
Success is not from without,
But from within.
And not the undermost,
And not the uppermost,
But he who labors most
Wisely shall win.

Hope and persistence —
These are the needs,
Coupled with patience,
    Whereby one succeeds.
Be not low-spirited ;
Though not inherited,
Heaven may be merited
    By faith and good deeds.

That is the talisman
    Leading us right ;
These are our jewels rare,
    Precious and bright.
Effort beneficent,
Though it be diffident,
Still is magnificent
    In the King's sight.

BOSTON STEREOTYPE FOUNDRY, 4 PEARL STREET.